WILL PRANCER BE READY FOR
THE HORSE SHOW?

Without any signal from Lisa, Prancer flew into the air, soaring over the low jump. Lisa had to grab on to Prancer's mane just to keep from falling off. While Lisa was startled at first, the feeling of flight was simply exhilarating. The fact that her horse wasn't doing just what she ought to be doing seemed insignificant compared to Prancer's incredible strength. Lisa sighed happily after the first jump and couldn't wait until the second.

"Lisa!" Max cried out.

"Isn't she something?" Lisa asked, grinning proudly.

"Well, I think she needs a little bit more work," Max stammered.

Carole and Stevie exchanged glances. They couldn't believe how oblivious Lisa was. . . .

THE SADDLE CLUB

SHOW HORSE

BONNIE BRYANT

A BANTAM SKYLARK BOOK®
NEW YORK · TORONTO · LONDON · SYDNEY · AUCKLAND

I would like to express my special thanks to Duffy Bump for her horse-show expertise and to Mark Kirschner for his common sense.

—B.B.H.

RL 5, 009–012

SHOW HORSE

A Bantam Skylark Book / December 1992

Skylark Books is a registered trademark of Bantam Books, a division of Bantam Doubleday Dell Publishing Group, Inc. Registered in U.S. Patent and Trademark Office and elsewhere.

"The Saddle Club" is a trademark of Bonnie Bryant Hiller. The Saddle Club design/logo, which consists of an inverted U-shapted design, a riding crop, and a riding hat is a trademark of Bantam Books.

ISBN 0-553-48072-3

Published simultaneously in the United States and Canada

Bantam Books are published by Bantam Books, a division of Bantam Doubleday Dell Publishing Group, Inc. Its trademark, consisting of the words "Bantam Books" and the portrayal of a rooster, is Registered in U.S. Patent and Trademark Office and in other countries. Marca Registrada. Bantam Books, 666 Fifth Avenue, New York, New York 10103.

PRINTED IN THE UNITED STATES OF AMERICA

CWO   0 9 8 7 6 5 4 3 2 1

CAROLE HANSON MOVED the cursor down the computer screen, flipping through the pages of bulletin-board notes before she got to the one she'd been waiting for. It read:

> With a pedal-bone fracture, it's probably a good idea to have the bone x-rayed again after seven months to make sure it's completely healed before the horse is ridden.
>
> Cam Nelson

Carole frowned at the computer screen, once again a little irritated that this Cam person seemed to have an answer for everything. Carole didn't think Cam knew what she was talking about this time, though.

Nobody had said anything about an X ray. Cam had to be wrong and Carole couldn't wait to tell her so. Carole didn't have time to answer that note now, though. Her riding class began in less than an hour, and she had to meet Pine Hollow Stables' vet, Judy Barker, for Prancer's final checkup before class. She exited from the program and turned off her computer.

Prancer was a Thoroughbred mare who had broken her pedal bone in the middle of a race. Although it was a fracture that would heal—in fact, it had already healed—the fracture had meant the end of Prancer's racing career. The horse had then been bought by Judy and Max Regnery, who owned the stable where Carole rode and where her own horse, Starlight, was boarded. Carole had helped take care of Prancer ever since the mare had arrived at Pine Hollow. Now Prancer was healed. It was time to get her back under saddle.

As Carole hurried to get ready to go to the stable, she thought about the computer and the modem her father had recently bought and what a change it had made in her life. It allowed her to access an interactive network with a BBS. She smiled to herself, realizing that a month ago she hadn't even known what any of those terms meant! Now she not only knew that an interactive network meant that she could share information with other members of the network, but she also corresponded with some of them regularly via the BBS—or Bulletin Board Service. Her first bulletin-board note had read:

I love horses. Anybody else do, too?

She'd gotten only a few responses, but it had been enough to get some interesting notes going back and forth. The person who wrote the most was a girl named Cam who seemed to know a lot. She sometimes seemed to know more than Carole did and Carole didn't always like that.

Carole knew a lot, too. She was crazy about horses. She was so crazy about them that she and her best friends from Pine Hollow, Stevie Lake and Lisa Atwood, had formed a group they called The Saddle Club. They had just two rules. All the members had to be horse crazy, and they all had to be willing to pitch in and help each other whenever help was needed. A lot of girls loved horses, but Carole thought she loved them the most. She wasn't certain what she was going to be when she grew up, but she was certain it was going to have something to do with horses.

She thought about them all the time. She thought about them as she left the house, as she climbed onto the bus, and as she walked from the bus stop to Pine Hollow. The only time she stopped thinking about them was when she was thinking about Cam Nelson, and that was actually thinking about horses, too. Carole wasn't sure how she felt about Cam. Carole was accustomed to being the girl who knew the most about horses. Cam apparently knew a lot, too, and Carole found herself wondering which one of them knew more. She never felt competitive with Lisa and

Stevie. She wondered what it was about Cam that made her feel competitive.

"Something's up, Carole," Stevie said, greeting her as soon as she arrived at Pine Hollow. "I just know it. I saw Max walking past the locker area a few minutes ago, and he had this big grin on his face." Her eyes were sparkling with excitement. "Come on, get dressed quickly. We've just got to find out what it is!" Stevie took Carole's arm, hurrying her into the locker area.

Carole let herself be led. The fact that Max, who was very serious around horses, was grinning, was a strong sign of some good news.

"I think it's just that he knows Prancer is ready for her first ride," Lisa said, tugging at her boot. Her feet had grown, and it was getting harder to get her boots on. "Oomph, there!" she declared triumphantly and then stood up. "We all know Prancer is this really valuable horse," Lisa began expanding on her theory. "Max is probably thrilled that he can now claim to have another Thoroughbred in his stable, right? I'm sure that's what he's happy about."

Lisa was a very logical person. She had the ability to analyze anything carefully. It was also an ability that consistently earned her straight A's on her report card, but it was also an ability that sometimes got her into trouble. She'd been known to get so carried away with her own analysis that she lost track of what was important. Her friends were always there to help her, though—just the way she helped them. That was one of the nicest things about The Saddle Club.

"Maybe Max is just happy about Prancer," Stevie said. "But that doesn't explain the fact that the grin was big enough to show his dimples. Something's got to be bigger than just Prancer for Max to let his dimples loose!"

Lisa and Carole giggled. Only Stevie would classify Max's happiness on a scale of whether his smile showed his dimples!

"Laugh if you want, but I'm right," Stevie assured them, tucking in her shirttail. "You'll see."

Lisa and Carole had spent enough time with Stevie to have a great deal of confidence in her hunches. They hoped she was right this time. It sounded like a nice hunch.

JUDY WAS ALREADY giving Prancer a final check when the girls arrived at the box stall. Lisa carried a saddle. Stevie had the bridle. Prancer greeted them warmly. The girls had learned long ago that horses' personalities were as different as people's. The Saddle Club had discovered that, like many racehorses, Prancer hadn't been bred for kindness and gentleness. She'd been bred for competitiveness and speed, and she had both those qualities. She tended to be abrupt and almost testy with adults, including Max and Judy. However, when it came to young people, she was as gentle and loving as could be.

The girls had speculated about what might have

caused that, but they knew they'd never know the real reason. Maybe it had to do with the fact that they were smaller than adults; maybe a young person had done her a kindness when Prancer was a filly; maybe an adult had done something cruel to her; or maybe it was none of those things. Whatever the reason was, it was true: One look at Carole, Lisa, and Stevie, and the mare seemed to relax and smile. She nuzzled Carole's neck. She sniffed at Lisa's hand—and wasn't disappointed, because Lisa did have a carrot for her. She nodded cheerfully when Stevie waved at her. Prancer was definitely in a good mood, too, just like Max.

"How does it look?" Carole asked Judy, who was already examining the mare's foot.

"Looks just fine, and I'd say she's as ready as can be for her test drive. Who's going to get the honors?" Judy asked.

"Lisa," Stevie said, and then explained. "She's the only one of us who hasn't had a chance to ride a Thoroughbred before." That was true. Carole had ridden several—including Prancer—and Stevie regularly rode a Thoroughbred named Topside.

"I agree," Carole said.

Lisa was thrilled. She didn't argue at all. She just began tacking up the mare.

As Carole watched Lisa prepare the horse, she was reminded of the note she'd gotten from Cam. It was still irking her. She asked Judy, "How do you know when the pedal bone is all healed?"

"Well, after this many months you can be fairly

certain that it's healed, but there are some other signs. First of all, she's not showing any indication of lameness. All the swelling is gone and has been for a while. There's no tenderness anywhere—I mean she doesn't flinch or pull back when I hold and examine her foot. That's enough to know it's healed."

That made Carole feel pretty good. What did that Cam know?

"And one more thing," Judy continued. "I x-rayed it yesterday, just to be sure. It's fine."

"Oh," Carole said. It was all she could muster. Cam had been right!

Lisa made a final adjustment on the stirrups and announced she was ready. Stevie opened the stall door, and Carole handed her the reins. Lisa proudly led Prancer to the door of the stable and stood on the mounting block to get into the saddle of the very tall horse. Then, following one of Pine Hollow's oldest traditions, she touched the good-luck horseshoe. No rider who had touched that before going out on a horse had ever been seriously hurt. Lisa didn't think she was going to need any more good luck than she already had, though. What could be better luck than just to have the chance to ride this beautiful bay Thoroughbred? She took a deep breath, sighed contentedly, and signaled Prancer to begin.

Prancer seemed eager. She had spent most of the last few months in a box stall or being walked sedately around a paddock. Now she had a rider on board, and everything seemed back to normal. Prancer almost sighed herself with contentment as they entered the schooling ring. She picked up an easy walk and within a few steps was trotting.

Lisa loved every step. She could barely believe the smooth and rapid gait. She hadn't even told Prancer to trot, and now the horse was doing it, exactly as she wanted her to. Maybe Prancer just knew!

Lisa posted to Prancer's trot, rising slightly with every other beat of the gait. She could feel the wind brush her hair, and she was only vaguely aware of the posts and rail of the fencing as she and her mount sailed by them. Even her friends, who stood and watched, faded into the blur that was the world beyond herself and Prancer. It was wonderful.

"Try a canter now," Judy said.

Lisa began to slide her outside foot back to ask Prancer for a canter, but the horse had heard the word and knew what it meant. Prancer's canter was, if possible, even better than her trot! Lisa sat easily in the saddle and rode with the gentle rocking motion, feeling completely at one with her horse.

"Now walk again," Judy said.

Lisa tightened up on her reins and sat more deeply in the saddle. It should have been enough to bring Prancer back to a trot and then a walk, but Prancer was having too much fun cantering.

She gripped more tightly with her legs and pulled gently on the reins. The canter slowed, but it didn't stop.

"A walk," Judy reminded her.

Quickly Lisa wrapped the reins around her hands to draw on them some more. She fairly pulled herself into the saddle by gripping more tightly with her legs, and then she yanked at the reins. Prancer got it. She slowed to a trot and then a walk. Lisa completed her circle of the ring and brought the horse to a stop where Judy and her friends were standing.

"That was *wonderful*!" she declared.

"We could tell already—by the gigantic grin on your face," Stevie joked.

"Doesn't she have marvelous gaits?" Carole asked.

"Absolutely," Lisa said.

"She was a little hard to control, though, wasn't she?" Judy asked.

Lisa shrugged. "Not really," she said. "Poor old Prancer's been cooped up for so long, she just wanted a chance to let it all out. I can understand that, can't you?"

"Oh, sure," Judy said. "I can understand it, but you can't let her get away with it."

"I know, I know," Lisa said. One of the things she both loved and hated about horseback riding was that everybody always seemed to notice everything she did wrong. She knew that almost all riding mistakes were mistakes made by riders, not horses. Prancer hadn't made the mistakes, she had. She hadn't tugged hard enough or fast enough to get Prancer to stop. It wouldn't happen again, though. And the next time she rode Prancer, it would be a perfect ride, because

9

there was absolutely no doubt in Lisa's mind that Prancer was a perfect horse!

"So how's the patient doing?" Max asked Judy as he joined the group. He hadn't been there to watch Lisa's ride, but he could tell it had been a success in Lisa's mind.

"The patient appears totally fit," Judy assured him. "Everything is clear and clean, and she's showing no signs of any lingering problems. I declare Prancer ready for a full load of work—riding and a lot more training."

"Well, that's just wonderful news," Max said. "And that means this is a day just full of good news. . . ."

Stevie glanced at her friends, and the look on her face was a clear I-told-you-so. She'd earned it.

"Yes?" Carole asked expectantly.

"I've just heard from the Briarwood Horse Show. They've invited me to send some of my students to compete the week after next."

"*Young* students?" Carole asked.

Max smiled. "Yes, young students. All the Junior riders are there by invitation, and they said I could pick four riders."

There was a moment of quiet while the information sank in. On the surface it sounded awfully good, but four was an ominous number. Would Max send all three of them? If not, then who? And who else?

Sitting in the saddle of a Thoroughbred horse, Lisa felt bold. "Any idea who you'll send?" she asked, speaking for them all.

"Well, I've had to think about it for a long time," Max said. "There are a lot of considerations. First of all, I need to send riders who have something to offer a competition. Then, I also want riders who will learn something from it. I told the man at Briarwood that I have this obstreperous threesome who think they know everything and who are always coming up with wild schemes and who get themselves into trouble and that they also talk a lot in class . . ."

"Max!" Stevie said. She just couldn't stand the suspense.

"But he said to send them along anyway. He promised to teach them a thing or two."

"You mean us, don't you?" Carole asked.

"Of course he means us!" Stevie snapped. "Who else is obstreperous and talks a lot in class?"

Max laughed and shook his head. "I told the man. He's been warned! So, right after class, come into my office and let's talk. But don't be late for class. It starts in ten minutes!"

Carole snapped a salute. "Aye, aye, sir," she said. Max clicked the heels of his boots together and left the girls to get ready.

There wasn't time to talk while they hurried to tack up their horses. They didn't want to be late for class. And they didn't want to talk in class because, although Max had joked about it a little bit, he really didn't like it, and this was no time to make him angry. Each of them found this frustrating because there was so *much* to say.

Carole was thrilled with the idea of competing at Briarwood. It was a very famous horse show. She didn't think her friends knew what an honor it was to be able to be there. She could hardly wait.

Stevie was itching to find out who the fourth young rider from Pine Hollow would be. There were a lot of pretty good riders, and there were some who weren't so good but who might do well in a beginner class. There was only one person she didn't want there: Veronica diAngelo. Veronica was a snobbish girl who owned a purebred Arabian and who cared more about her horse's pedigree than about her own riding skills. In spite of that, Stevie had to admit that Veronica was a pretty good rider.

Lisa was still so excited about her ride on Prancer that it was almost all she could think about. She'd been assigned another horse, Barq, to ride for class, though she would have preferred Prancer. She kept trying to pretend that Barq *was* Prancer. Barq was a perfectly nice horse, but Barq was no Prancer. Still, if she closed her eyes . . .

"Lisa? Are you asleep?" Stevie asked just before they entered the arena for class.

"No, just dreaming," she told her friend, and it was true. She was dreaming about the magic moment when she and Prancer would enter the ring at the Briarwood Horse Show.

STEVIE GROANED INWARDLY. It would have been impolite to do it out loud, but it was very tempting. She was standing in Max's office, between her two best friends. Next to Lisa stood the fourth member of the Pine Hollow team going to Briarwood—Veronica di-Angelo. Max didn't seem to notice Stevie's unhappiness. At least he wasn't paying any attention to it. He was very busy explaining what would happen at the horse show.

"All right now, here's how it works," he began. "You are all Intermediate riders in the Junior Division. There are five different classes for you each, and each class stresses different skills and talents. Don't assume that because you're good riders you will do well in all of the classes. That's not always the case."

Carole thought he was talking to her. She did think of herself as a good rider and hoped she would do well in all the classes, but she wasn't sure she *expected* it of herself.

Lisa's mind leapt in another direction. She felt that Max was telling her that although she was the newest rider of the group, it didn't mean she couldn't succeed at the show. She smiled to herself, glad that Max was giving her such assurances.

Stevie, on the other hand, thought it was interesting that Max had found such a subtle way to tell Veronica she wasn't going to sweep the ribbons. After all, nothing spurred Stevie to excellence like competition. This show was going to be a wonderful opportunity for Stevie and her friends to humiliate Veronica!

Veronica just stood and smiled smugly while Max spoke.

"The first class of the day for you will be Fitting and Showing. You'll lead your horses into the ring without any saddles on them. The judges will be looking for grooming, conformation, and manners. The second class is Equitation. In that, you will be showing your riding skills. You'll follow instructions about gaits, directions, turns, and gait changes. These will be many of the same things we cover every week in class. If you have been listening to me, rather than daydreaming or talking among yourselves, you will do well in this class."

Lisa squirmed uncomfortably. She'd daydreamed a lot in the last class. Max had had to tell her twice to trot, and he'd spoken to her several times about keeping her heels down. Although he often told her she was making a lot of progress as a rider, he still managed to point out four or five of her riding faults at a time! She was going to have to work hard to be worthy of this horse show. She promised herself she'd stop daydreaming altogether. As of now.

"The next class is a Pleasure class. That's just what it sounds like. There are no tricky maneuvers expected, just good, solid riding and a good relationship between horse and rider. This is the class where that's the most important. If you work well with your horse and if you both enjoy it, you'll do well in this one."

In spite of her vow only a few seconds earlier, Lisa's mind wandered at the mention of the word "pleasure." Prancer was a pleasure. Prancer was wonderful, and riding Prancer was a joy. . . .

". . . over poles and around cones, as if they were actual obstacles . . ."

"What?" Lisa asked, startled back to reality.

"Trail class," Max said patiently. "It takes place in a ring, but the route that you ride will be set up like a pretend trail. There may be a few low fences—perhaps six inches high—just so the judges can see how you prepare your horses for obstacles like that."

"Oh," Lisa said. She wondered if she'd missed anything and made a note to ask Stevie and Carole about it later.

"And then, finally, there is the Jumping class. It's hunter jumping, and the jumps won't be over three and a half feet. What the judges are looking for here is style. They want to see you riding at an even gait, going over the jumps smoothly, with takeoff an appropriate distance from the jump—again, everything you've learned in class with me over the past few years. I'll schedule some special prep classes for the four of you before we go so you can each put your best foot forward at Briarwood. I want you to remember a few things, though, and one above all. This may be a chance for you to show off skills and win a ribbon or two, but most of all, it is a chance for you each to learn. You will learn from your own mistakes, and you will learn from other people's talents and skills. Keep your eyes and your minds and your hearts open at all times."

He looked at each of them solemnly as he spoke. With that look, the girls found themselves readjusting their initial reactions to going to the show. Carole wasn't so sure then that she would do well in every event. Stevie wasn't positive she'd do better than Veronica. Lisa decided that she had to find a way to surpass everybody's expectations.

"Now then, you will each need a permission slip signed by your parents. Here you go," he said, handing them out. "I'll need them back by next week, at the latest. And I need you each to tell me officially which horse you intend to ride in the show since you are entered as a pair. Carole?"

"Starlight, of course. It'll be a challenge for him, and I know he could use some more training, but I think the experience will be good for him, as well as me."

"I agree," Max said. He jotted down the name.

"Veronica?"

"Garnet," she answered. "She's so beautiful, she's sure to catch the judges' attention."

"Yes," Max said. Stevie had the sneaking suspicion *he* wanted to groan then.

"Stevie?"

"Topside. He knows more about horse shows than I do."

"I agree," Max said. "And Lisa?"

It seemed like the chance of a lifetime to Lisa. Without hesitation she spoke her answer. "Prancer," she said.

Max looked at her. For a second Lisa thought he was going to object. Carole began to speak, but Max held up his hand to silence her. "Interesting," he said. Then he nodded. "Well, then, Prancer it is. All right, I'll see you all next time. Bring those permission forms."

They'd been dismissed.

"ARE YOU CRAZY?" Stevie asked. She didn't have the patience for diplomacy. The three girls were on their way to their favorite hangout, an ice-cream shop called TD's, for a much-needed talk about the upcoming horse show. Stevie, however, couldn't hold her thoughts in for one minute longer. "You can't ride Prancer in the horse show!"

"Sure I can," Lisa said. "Max said it was all right."

"Well maybe he's crazy, too," Stevie said.

"Why? What's wrong with riding Prancer?" Lisa challenged her friend.

"Everything!" Stevie said. "Prancer is a very valuable horse—"

"You think I'm not good enough to ride a Thoroughbred like you are?" Lisa asked. She was getting really angry at Stevie, and it wasn't like her to do that.

"That's not what I meant," Stevie said.

"It's what you said!"

"No, you didn't let me finish saying what I was going to say," Stevie persisted, trying to get her point across. "Prancer is valuable and beautiful, but all of her training has been for speed and none of it for horse-show skills. She's just not ready."

"Oh, come on," Lisa said. "How many times have you two told me that a horse is only as good as the rider in the saddle? Prancer can do anything!"

"Sure she can," Stevie began. "With the proper training . . ."

Lisa scowled at Stevie. Then Carole came to her rescue.

"Prancer certainly is a wonderful horse," Carole began carefully.

"See? I told you, Stevie!" Lisa said. "All you have to do is try riding her. I'm telling you, it was like love at first sight between us."

"I know the feeling," Carole said. "Remember, I've ridden Prancer."

The girls continued toward the ice-cream shop in silence. It was unusual for there to be a disagreement among them, but that was clearly the case now. Stevie and Carole were worried about Lisa's decision while Lisa was convinced she was right. In spite of her conviction, Lisa didn't like being at odds with her friends. She decided to change the subject. They entered TD's and took their favorite booth at the back of the shop.

"None of this may matter anyway," Lisa said, sliding across the smooth red plastic of the seat. "The hardest part of the horse show may be getting my mother to sign the permission form."

Stevie's eyes lit up. This sort of thing was right up her alley and had the sound of a real Saddle Club project. Her mind raced.

"Got it," she said, reaching for the menu. "Have your father sign the form."

"I've been trying that tactic for years," Lisa said. "My parents figured it out the first time I tried to get an allowance from each of them. I can't split their ranks. Try again."

Stevie was only too willing to try. "Okay, then, there's the burnt-out light bulb ploy. You can only use it once, though."

This was definitely classic Stevie Lake. Lisa could feel the tension drain from among the three of them, and she was very relieved about it. These were her two best friends in the whole world. She didn't like being angry at them or having the feeling that she couldn't trust them.

"Okay, the light bulb thing works this way: All of the light bulbs in the room burn out at once—really what you do is flip the circuit breaker, and later you tell them you were ironing and making toast at the same time and you're awfully sorry—and just at that moment, you ask your mom for her autograph. Then you give her the permission form. She's so flattered you want her autograph that she doesn't even look at the paper. . . ."

"Has this actually ever worked for you?" Carole asked in disbelief.

"Not for me, but it's definitely worth a try. Besides, my parents are always suspicious of me. The minute I'd say I was ironing, they'd know something was up."

"What'll you have?" the waitress asked the three girls. She dutifully wrote down the two hot-fudge sundaes that Carole and Lisa wanted and then grimaced as she steeled herself to take Stevie's order.

"Oh, uh, coffee ice cream," Stevie began. "Then I want some maple-walnut syrup and blackberry preserve, plus peanut-butter crunchies and, naturally, whipped cream. Oh, don't forget the maraschino cherry this time, will you? I think you forgot it last time."

"And you noticed?" the waitress asked. Carole and Lisa stifled smiles. Since Stevie's sundaes always combined so many strange ingredients, it *was* amazing that she had noticed one was missing—even if it was the maraschino cherry.

As soon as the waitress was gone, Stevie leaned

forward conspiratorially. "I think they do that some-times just to check on me," she said to her friends. "As a matter of fact, I think they have bets about it!"

Lisa and Carole were quite sure Stevie was right, because they would have done exactly the same thing if they'd had to make up the sundaes that Stevie invented!

"Okay, now, back to business—you could just try forging your mother's signature," Stevie suggested.

"I could," Lisa said, "but she'd find out. No, the trick here is going to be to get her to sign it and want to sign it."

"Harder, much harder," Stevie said. That didn't mean she was defeated. Just that the challenge was going to be more fun.

"You could ask Max for help," Carole suggested.

Stevie gave her a withering look. Asking adults for help when a mischievous and sneaky method was available was out of the question. She scratched her head.

"Three hot-fudge sundaes," the waitress announced.

"That's not what I—"

"I know. I've brought you what you ordered," the woman assured Stevie. "I just can't bring myself to say what's in it. Here, eat it."

The concoction appeared. Stevie looked at it and smiled. "Oh, good, you gave me two maraschino cher-ries this time!"

"Trying to make up for last time," the waitress said.

Then she hurried away before she had to watch Stevie eat any of it.

For the next few minutes, the girls were quite occupied with their sundaes. They couldn't even talk about horses, but their minds weren't far from the subject. As they ate, each thought about Briarwood and how wonderful the show would be.

"I'm just going to have to get my mother to sign it!" Lisa blurted out. "I mean, they have to let me and Prancer ride in the show!"

"Oh, they will," Carole said. She couldn't imagine how a parent could refuse to give permission for something that exciting. Certainly her father would be as excited as she was.

Lisa took a final spoonful of her sundae and then took a big gulp of cold water. "I'd better get going," she said, fishing enough money out of her wallet to cover the sundae and a tip for the poor waitress. "I've got some work to do—on my parents."

With that she stood up and waved good-bye to her friends. "See you Monday—and I'll talk to you before then. For sure."

"For sure," Stevie agreed.

"Bye," Carole said.

"I still think she's crazy," Stevie said to Carole when she was sure Lisa was out of earshot. "Prancer is no more ready to ride in that horse show than my pet turtle is."

"You don't have a pet turtle," Carole said.

"That's what I mean," said Stevie.

22

"But Max agreed—"

"I wonder why," Stevie mused. "He usually has his reasons."

"He usually does," Carole agreed. "So let's you and me worry about other things. There's something I want to ask you about. What do you think about working on jump training with a lunge line?"

Stevie thought for a moment. A lunge line was a long leash attached to a bridle on a horse and could be used for training. It gave the trainer a different perspective on the horse's movement than being in the saddle did. "Sounds good to me," she said.

"I don't know," Carole said thoughtfully. The reason she was asking Stevie about it was that Cam had suggested it and Carole was still annoyed that Cam had been right about the need to x-ray Prancer. On a computer note Carole had told Cam that jumping was best done in the saddle, but now she wanted Stevie's opinion. "Don't you think it's better to practice jumping in the saddle?" she asked Stevie.

"Most of the time, sure," Stevie agreed. "But using a lunge sometimes would be helpful. You've lunged Starlight to keep his gaits even. Why not do it for jumping?"

"Maybe," Carole said, but she didn't like saying it. Although she'd asked Stevie's opinion, what she had really wanted was for Stevie to agree with her. She wasn't too pleased with the fact that Stevie seemed to be siding with Cam—even though Stevie didn't have the faintest idea in the world that Cam even existed!

Stevie looked at her oddly. She wondered what was going on. But Carole's face told her she wasn't going to get any more information, so she changed the subject.

"What do you think Veronica will do to try to mess up the horse show for the rest of us?"

Now there was a topic they could both enjoy discussing at length!

3

"REALLY," STEVIE SAID into the telephone. "We're going to be at Briarwood! Isn't it great?" She was curled up on her bed, talking to her boyfriend, Phil Marston. Since he was a rider, too—in fact, he even owned his own horse—she loved talking with him about riding as much as she loved talking about it with Lisa and Carole.

"All three of you?" Phil Marston asked. "Competing against one another?"

"What?" Stevie said, startled by his comment. "I hadn't thought of it that way. I was thinking of it as *us* competing against everyone else. . . ."

"That's not how it works," Phil said. "I've been in horse shows. Believe me, when you're out in the ring in a class, or performing individually, you're alone.

25

You and your horse are the only two creatures on the earth that matter—except for the judges, of course. I know you, Stevie. You'll want to win."

Will I? Stevie asked herself. Would she want to win so badly that she'd want to beat her two best friends? She didn't want to think about that.

"You're all good riders, of course," Phil continued. "But I have my favorite of the three of you."

"You do?" Stevie asked coyly. "And just who is your favorite?"

"Well, I'll give you a hint. . . . ," he began. Stevie fluffed up her pillow and leaned back on it to relax. She was having a really good time. But she also couldn't help wondering how much she would tell Carole and Lisa about her talk with Phil when she saw them on Monday.

"IT'S A REALLY important horse show," Lisa said to her parents. "It's a regional AHSA show, and it's rated A-minus."

"What does that mean?"

"It means that even just competing in it is important, Mom," Lisa explained carefully. "And winning in it would be even more important."

"Horse shows are dangerous," her mother countered. "You've even said so yourself. Why, that friend of yours who was riding in New York—Dorothy what's her name?—didn't she get badly hurt?"

"Dorothy DeSoto," Lisa said patiently. Dorothy was a former student of Max's who had been successful in international competitions. Her career had been cut short by a freakish accident at a horse show in New York. A careless woman in the front row of the audience had spooked Dorothy's horse. "She wasn't hurt all that badly," Lisa continued. "I mean she had to go to the hospital and all, but what her doctor said was that she couldn't risk being hurt again. The next time would be much more serious. So she had to give up riding."

"Well, I don't want that to happen to you."

"It won't, Mom. I promise," Lisa said. She hoped she was being convincing, but the look on her mother's face didn't encourage her.

"Of course it won't happen to you," said Mrs. Atwood. "Because you won't be competing."

"Dad?" Lisa implored.

Her father shrugged. "I don't know," he began hesitantly.

That sounded to Lisa like an opening, and she took advantage of it, Stevie-style. "See, Mom? Dad's in favor of it—"

"I, uh," her father protested.

"No, he isn't," Mrs. Atwood snapped. "He knows that riding is dangerous and competing is even more dangerous. There's no way he would want you to hurt yourself, is there, dear?"

"I, uh—"

"See, Mom? He wants me to have this wonderful opportunity to ride with the best. It's a way I can learn from the best. Riding is a safe activity when you follow

27

the instructions you've had drilled into you, and Max Regnery has done an awful lot of drilling, and he says I'm a good student and you know that's true because I've always been a good student, and I always get A's at school and it's no different at Pine Hollow, where I work hard and study hard and try to do my best, and Max and my other teachers and my friends tell me I've learned an awful lot, which includes riding safely—" She had to stop to take a breath. Her mother was too surprised by the outpouring to interrupt. Lisa didn't have a clue if her flood of words was having any positive effect on her mother, but she knew that as long as she kept on talking, her mother wouldn't have a chance to say no.

". . . and besides, Max would never ask any of the four of us to do anything that wasn't safe because—"

"Four?" Mrs. Atwood asked, interrupting.

"Yes, sure, I told you, didn't I?"

"No."

Then Lisa saw a light. "It's me, Stevie, Carole, and Veronica diAngelo."

"Veronica diAngelo?"

Lisa nodded, glad to be silent for a moment and realizing that this might be the opportunity she'd been hoping for. Nobody liked Veronica diAngelo. Even Mrs. Atwood knew that she was a spoiled brat. But nobody could contend that Veronica wasn't proper. If Veronica's parents were willing to let her compete in the horse show, Mrs. Atwood would certainly have to consider it. It was a start.

*   *   *

CAROLE WATCHED THE screen of her computer intently.

ENTER PASSWORD

She entered it. The screen blinked and switched; a colorful picture appeared. That held no interest for Carole. All she wanted was to get to the kids' bulletin board and see if there was any news from Cam. Most of all, she could hardly wait to tell Cam that she was going to be in a horse show. That would impress her!

She scrolled through the messages until she got to the most recent. It was from Cam.

> *I had class today. We worked on leg yielding. I didn't do it well. Anybody know anything about this that I don't?*
>
> *Cam Nelson*

Sure, Carole knew some things about leg yielding. She knew it was a way to have your horse move both forward and sideways at the same time, sort of a diagonal stride, without having his legs cross one another and always keeping himself facing forward. It involved giving subtle but strong signals to a horse, and it could be tricky. Carole wanted to try to help. She cleared her screen, switching to "Send," and began writing.

> *The only trick that's ever worked for me in leg yielding is to keep my head and my eyes faced*

29

absolutely straight ahead, just the way I want my horse to face. Then I use my inside leg carefully, keeping it at exactly the same angle I want the horse to have—somehow sort of both forward and sideways. Good luck with it.

Carole Hanson
P.S. I got some great news today at class: I'm going to be in a horse show in two weeks. Stand by everybody out there in computerland. I'm going to need every bit of help I can get over the next four-teen days!

She pressed the keys to send her message and then returned to the bulletin board to see if any other messages had come in earlier. That was when she noticed that Cam's note had been put up only a few minutes earlier. There was a blinking of the screen and her own note appeared. Modern technology was amazing!

Carole browsed. She found a note from a young rider about feeding schedules, and she made a mental note to answer that. Feeding was something she knew a lot about. Then she returned to her own note and was surprised to find that already it was not the last note on the board.

Carole? Are you there?

It was from Cam! She was on the computer at the same time Carole was. This was like having a phone conversation!

I'm here, Carole typed in quickly.

Cam quickly responded.

> *I saw your note about the horse show in two weeks. It must be Briarwood—right? Well, it looks like we're actually going to meet. I'll be at Briarwood, too, probably even competing against you. What classes are you going to be in?*

Carole stared numbly at the screen. She was actually going to meet Cam—the girl who seemed to know it all. Why did this bother her so much? She had a feeling it was because she was so used to being the one who knew the most about horses—even among the rest of The Saddle Club. What if it turned out that Cam was a better rider and knew more than she did? What difference would it make that Carole could give a hint about leg yielding, if she couldn't win a higher-place ribbon than Cam? What if . . . ? She didn't even want to think about the other "ifs," and she had the odd feeling that if she didn't answer Cam's note right away, Cam would know that she was nervous and insecure. Above all, she couldn't let Cam see that.

Carole switched screens to send a reply.

> *The show is Briarwood. And I can't wait. There will be four of us there from Pine Hollow, including three of us from the club that I told you*

about, The Saddle Club. We're all going to be competing in Intermediate classes in . . .

What if Cam was in Advanced? Could she stand it? Carole couldn't believe how nervous she was all of a sudden. She forced herself to continue typing.

. . . Fitting and Showing, Equitation, Pleasure, Trail, and Jumping. What about you?

She tabbed to "Send," pressed "Enter," then waited. It didn't take long to receive an answer from Cam:

Same here. That's pretty exciting!

That wasn't quite the word Carole would have used. But then, she wasn't sure what word she would have used. One thing was certain, though. Briarwood was going to be no ordinary horse show.

THE NEXT SADDLE Club meeting took place at Pine Hollow. The three girls met at the stable on Monday. Since Carole went to the stable nearly every day to take care of Starlight, it was always convenient for Stevie and Lisa to join her there. But Mrs. Reg, Max's mother, hated the sight of young girls hanging around a stable doing nothing more than chatting, so before they knew it, she'd assign them tasks. At least they could talk while they were working.

Today Carole groomed Starlight while Stevie and Lisa mucked out the stall next to his.

"Phil says he's sure we're all going to do very well at Briarwood," Stevie said. That wasn't exactly what Phil had said, but it was as close as she wanted to share with her friends.

"*If* we all get to Briarwood," Lisa said, sighing. "I talked to my mother. I think I made some progress with her, but there's no telling for sure until her signature is on the form."

"Oh, she'll sign it," Carole said. "There's no way she's going to keep you from having such a wonderful growing and learning experience."

"I just hope you're right," said Lisa. "And what was it you were saying about this person you met on your computer? What's her name?"

"Cam," Carole said. "Cam Nelson. She's a pretty good rider, I guess. I mean, she always seems to know things—"

"What's all that talk going on there?" Mrs. Reg said, interrupting the conversation. "Aren't you three supposed to be *doing* something?" she asked pointedly.

For a second it occurred to Stevie to point out that they *were* doing something until she realized that both she and Lisa had been using their pitchforks to prop up their elbows for quite a few minutes. Since that had certainly come to Mrs. Reg's attention, she decided to try something else.

"Yes," she said. "We're supposed to be tacking up Starlight, Topside, and Prancer to take them out on a trail ride, which is going to be a sort of practice ride for the Trail class at Briarwood. Didn't Max tell you?"

Mrs. Reg stifled a smile. She knew Stevie was fibbing, but Stevie always did it so charmingly that she got away with it more often than not. This was going to be one of those times.

34

"He must have forgotten to mention it to me," Mrs. Reg countered, "but if you're going out on a ride, you'd better get out there quickly. It'll start getting dark in an hour or two. . . ." Then she winked at Stevie.

"We'll be back before dark. Promise," Stevie said. Then she and her friends practically raced to the locker area, where they changed very quickly into the spare riding clothes that they always kept at the stable, before dashing to the tack room. There wasn't a second to waste, especially if they wanted to use up every minute of daylight.

Fifteen minutes later the threesome met at the door that led out the back of the stable. Each touched the good-luck horseshoe, and they were on their way, long before Mrs. Reg had a chance to change her mind.

"Whew!" Stevie declared when they began their trek across the meadow behind Pine Hollow.

"I don't know how you do it," Carole said. "I mean there we were, having a really nice time just chatting in the stable, and you somehow managed to think of a way to make it even better!"

Stevie smiled at the compliment. "My pleasure," she said. "Definitely."

Her friends agreed with that.

The girls rode in single file. Carole was first and Stevie was at the rear. Lisa, as the least experienced rider, was in the middle. Lisa was thrilled to be riding Prancer on a trail ride. Although she loved riding in any form, her favorite was definitely in the open on a trail. It seemed like the natural way to ride. Horses, after all, were creatures of nature, and being in the open always seemed to bring out the best in them.

Prancer tugged at her bit. Lisa relaxed the reins a little. Prancer tugged some more.

"Tighten up on those reins," Stevie said from behind.

"The bit seems to be bothering her," Lisa explained. "She seems to want it looser."

"Naturally," Stevie said. "They always do. That way the horse can be in charge, but you're the one in the saddle, not Prancer. You have to be in charge."

"Right," Lisa said. She drew in on the leather and made the reins taut. Prancer nodded her head in protest. Lisa released it a little.

"Ready to trot?" Carole asked from her position in the lead.

"You bet!" Lisa said. Then before she could even readjust the pressure of her legs on Prancer to tell her to trot, the horse picked up the faster gait.

Half of Lisa's mind told her that was a bad thing. She knew that it just wasn't a good idea to let the horse decide when to trot. The other half shrugged it off. After all, trotting *was* what she wanted Prancer to do, wasn't it?

Once again Lisa was thrilled with the fluid motion of the Thoroughbred horse. Even though Prancer hadn't been bred for her trot, it was smooth and speedy. It nearly took Lisa's breath away. The horse seemed to feel the utter joy of motion, of the outdoors, of the field. She sniffed eagerly at the fresh wind that filled her nostrils and watched as the countryside sped by her. Her stride lengthened, her pace quickened.

"Pull her back," Stevie said. "You're riding too close to Carole."

Lisa had barely noticed that Prancer had inched up on her friend's horse, but when she did, she couldn't help smiling to herself. She was riding a racehorse— one whose very breeding had been designed for competition. Prancer would always want to be first. That would suit Lisa just fine.

Ahead, Carole raised her hand and pointed forward. It was a signal that she was preparing to canter. Starlight began cantering, and that was enough for Prancer. With a sudden burst Prancer began cantering, too, and then without any warning broke into a gallop. If she'd been bred to race at a trot, she'd been bred to win at a gallop.

While Lisa could ignore Prancer's bad manners on trotting without a signal, then gaining on Starlight in single file, she couldn't ignore the fact that her horse was galloping and she hadn't even told her to canter.

Instantly she responded by gripping tightly with her knees, pulling as firmly on the reins as she could and she sat deeply in the saddle.

Although she couldn't ignore Prancer, it seemed that Prancer could ignore her. If possible, the horse seemed to be going even faster! Within seconds Prancer had passed in front of Starlight and was racing across the field toward the woods. It was where Lisa wanted to go, but it definitely wasn't how Lisa wanted to get there. She held herself firmly in the saddle and tugged on the reins. Prancer shook her head in rebellion, and kept on.

"Hold her back!" Carole called.

"Stop her!" Stevie yelled.

Lisa tried everything again. She even said, "Whoa," but Prancer, it appeared, didn't speak English. Lisa couldn't believe how ineffectual her efforts were. And then, as she neared the woods, Prancer slowed and stopped. Lisa sighed with relief and shook her head in anger.

It shouldn't have happened. She knew better. She had allowed Prancer to get the upper hand and take over. There was no way a horse who thought herself to be in charge was going to pay any attention to her rider.

"Are you okay?" Carole asked. She could see that Lisa's face was flushed with embarrassment.

"No," Lisa answered. "I just broke every rule the most amateur rider in the world knows and let my horse run away with me."

"Prancer, you bad girl!" Stevie chided when she got to her friend.

"It wasn't Prancer, it was me," Lisa said, reflexively defending the valuable horse. "I never should have let her trot without signaling her."

"Well, maybe," Stevie said. "But it seems to me that you paid too high a price for a little slip."

"Absolutely," Lisa agreed. "It was all my fault."

"No, that's not what I meant," Stevie said. "I mean, you did make a mistake, but at some point before a gallop, Prancer should have listened to you. You gave her every signal in the book. She just wasn't paying any attention."

"I can't blame her," Lisa said. "I just wasn't doing it right."

"You weren't?" Carole asked. She was a little surprised. "You used all your aids, didn't you? Your hands, legs, seat?"

"Yes," Lisa said. "But not enough, or it would have worked, so it's my fault." Then she really surprised her friends. She leaned forward in the saddle and patted Prancer. "There, there, girl," she said. "I'll try to do better next time. I won't let you down or confuse you again. I promise. I'll do better for you."

Carole and Stevie exchanged looks. Each was thinking the same thing. Lisa was, for some reason, blaming herself for something her horse was doing. Lisa had done almost everything right. It was Prancer who wasn't paying attention to her training here, not Lisa.

The other thought they had in common was that Lisa was not in a mood to hear that. She was only able to blame herself, and there was no way she'd accept the fact that Prancer had simply misbehaved. There wasn't even any point in trying to tell her that. But, Stevie decided, there was a point in making sure that it didn't happen again right away.

"You know, I just remembered that I've got a science experiment to write up tonight. I don't think we should take a long trail ride," Stevie said.

Lisa was too preoccupied with her own shortcomings as a rider to consider the fact that Stevie never, ever would stop riding for something as minor as a major school assignment. All Lisa wanted to do now was get back to the stable and try to figure out how to be worthy of the wonderful horse she so badly wanted to ride.

"Okay," she agreed. The three of them returned at a stately walk and in an uncomfortable silence. Each girl had her own thoughts and didn't find them easy to share with her friends. And this wasn't the way it usually went for The Saddle Club.

As they arrived at the stable, the fourth Pine Hollow entrant in the Briarwood Horse Show greeted them.

"Practicing your trail skills?" Veronica asked in obvious disbelief.

It was just what Stevie, Lisa, and Carole needed. They had issues that separated them from time to time, but one thing that always brought them back together was their feelings about Veronica diAngelo.

"Oh, yes," Stevie said sweetly. "We thought if we worked as hard as possible over the next two weeks we might, just possibly, get to be as good as you are in at least one event."

"I guess I always have been pretty good at trail riding," Veronica said, looking a little surprised at Stevie's remark. "It's going to be rough on you three, too, because, after all, I'm well prepared for a show like Briarwood. It's the kind of place where you find the best people. . . ."

The girls knew that Veronica did not mean the best *riders*. She meant the most socially acceptable people. The idea that class and money meant anything when you were riding in a horse show was so ridiculous that Stevie just had to say something to keep from laughing.

"Well, we're counting on you and your background and experience to help us all on that score, Veronica," she said with all the sincerity she could muster.

"I'll do my best," Veronica said. Then, suddenly suspecting that Stevie didn't mean every word she'd uttered, Veronica backed down a bit. "Naturally, I can't teach you everything—there are some things that you just have to know. . . ."

"Naturally," Carole said. "Survival of the fittest and all that."

"Exactly," Veronica said, as if she knew what it meant.

Prancer began dancing uneasily then, shifting quickly from left to right. Lisa pulled back on the reins to calm her, but it didn't seem to work.

"I think we'd better untack now," Carole said, realizing that Lisa ought to be getting off Prancer before the mare began acting up again. Since untacking meant work, Veronica took that line as an opportunity to make her exit. She would not want to be expected to help.

"That girl," Stevie said when Veronica seemed to be out of earshot. "Do you believe her?"

"I never have," Carole said, dismounting. "She's one of a kind, and that's just fine with me."

Carole held Prancer's reins while Lisa dismounted. The mare stood relatively still, and Lisa was finally safely on the ground.

"You okay with untacking her?" Carole asked.

"Of course I am," Lisa assured her. "We've got a lot to talk about."

"Yes, we do," Stevie said seriously.

"Not you and me. Me and Prancer," Lisa said. Then, without hesitation, she led the Thoroughbred mare to her stall.

Stevie and Carole exchanged looks. "Later," Carole said ominously. Stevie agreed.

Lisa clipped Prancer to a set of cross-ties by her stall and began untacking and grooming her.

"I'll do better by you over the next two weeks," she whispered to the mare as she worked. "I won't forget to tell you what to do. You're such a wonderful horse; you're probably used to better riders. Right now I'm what you've got, but I promise to make it possible for you to win blue ribbons at the horse show. Really."

For the first time since Lisa had gotten into Prancer's saddle, the mare seemed to relax. Lisa was sure her words had soothed the animal. Now if only she could make her actions match those words.

Around the corner of the stable, Carole gave Starlight's rump an affectionate slap. He nodded in return.

She removed his saddle and when she saw him in his bridle alone, it made her think of a lunge line. That, in turn, made her think of Cam. She'd meant to tell her friends about Cam, but then Mrs. Reg had interrupted and she'd forgotten to get back to the subject. It seemed odd to her now that she was actually going to meet Cam—meet the girl who knew so much about horses. Did she know more than Carole? Carole didn't even like asking herself the question, so she asked Starlight as she began his grooming.

"What do you say, boy? Is Cam a better rider than I am?"

At first there was no answer at all. Then a fly landed on Starlight's ear. He twitched it. The fly didn't budge. Starlight shook his head vigorously.

Carole smiled to herself. "Good answer," she said. She returned to her brushing, barely aware that the fly now circled her own head.

She wasn't sure Starlight had exactly answered her question, but she thought maybe it was a sign. Starlight, however, seemed much more interested in how good the brush felt on his coat.

Stevie was out in the ring with Topside, who had seemed to need a cool-down walk when they got back from their ride. The two of them were circling the schooling ring at a gentle walk. Stevie checked his respirations periodically. He was fine—just needed to walk a little longer. Stevie had something on her mind and needed to talk.

"Now listen up," she said to her horse. "You don't

have to take anything old Veronica says seriously. She thinks she's bound to win it all at the horse show because she's got this beautiful horse named Garnet. Well, so what? Everybody knows Garnet is beautiful, but she's not as well trained as you. Veronica hasn't worked for what she's learned, and she's not going to start, much less finish her training in the next two weeks. You and I have worked long and hard together. We're going to see some blue for our efforts. I promise," she said.

Stevie knew that she was a good rider. She had a good chance to succeed at the show. She also had the advantage of riding a first-rate horse. She would surely do well at the show. She might even do better than her friends. Then she stopped to think about how that would make her feel. Carole and Lisa were her best friends in the whole world. Did she really want to beat them at Briarwood? Yes, she realized. She did.

"POOR VERONICA," LISA said, almost sighing, at the dinner table on Friday night. It was about the last chance she was going to have to get her mother to sign the permission slip, and she'd planned her attack very carefully.

"Veronica? What about Veronica?" Mrs. Atwood asked.

"Well, she's got this idea that she's going to win everything at the horse show," Lisa said.

"She's very good, isn't she?" Mrs. Atwood asked. Lisa was always surprised that her mother never seemed to get the message about Veronica. Sure, Veronica was a pretty good rider, but she wasn't anywhere near as good as she thought she was, or as good as she believed her social status made her.

"She's pretty good, Mom," Lisa said. "But Garnet, Veronica's horse, isn't the best horse from Pine Hollow."

"Really?" Mrs. Atwood asked. "And just who has a better horse than Veronica diAngelo?"

"Actually, Mom," Lisa said, "the horse I am going to be riding is a better horse than Garnet."

"Yours? You mean one of Max's plain stable horses is more valuable than what the diAngelos bought for their daughter?"

"Sure, and it's no fluke. Prancer—that's the horse I'm riding now—is a Thoroughbred. She was a racehorse, and she was having a great career until she broke a bone. That's when Max bought her."

"Some run-down old nag?"

"No, Mom," Lisa said patiently. "Prancer is a young mare with outstanding bloodlines. She just has a weakness in her feet that makes her a poor risk for racing. She's going to be fabulous in the show ring."

"Really?"

Lisa liked the sound of that. It indicated that her mother was actually listening to her.

"What are you working on with the horse now?" her father asked. Lisa liked the sound of that, too. It was typical of her father that he would understand there were real issues about being in a horse show, issues more important than comparing the value of her horse to Veronica diAngelo's.

"Today we were working on trail skills," Lisa answered. "One of the classes is a Trail class, and although it will all take place in a ring . . ."

She went on to describe the event as carefully as possible, saying she thought it was interesting that the class tried to imitate natural obstacles in an artificial environment, the ring.

"It's the same thing with the Jumping class," she said. "In that, a fox-hunting course is created in the ring. Some of the jumps are made to look like regular natural obstacles, too, with bushes and sometimes even some water. It's going to be neat." Then she realized that she'd been doing an awful lot of talking. The idea here was to allow her parents to think about what she'd said, and that was hard to do if she was still talking. Automatically she silenced herself and concentrated on the rice on her plate.

"You've done a lot of work on this, haven't you?" Mr. Atwood asked.

She nodded. "It's important to me, Dad," she said truthfully.

"I can tell," he said. Then he looked at his wife. "Eleanor? I think we need to consider Lisa's wishes here seriously—at least as seriously as she has."

"Yes, Richard," she said. "I mean, if her horse is actually better than Veronica diAngelo's . . ."

"Mom, I've got an idea," Lisa said. This was her trump card, and she was ready to lay it on the table. "Why don't you come to class with me tomorrow? You can watch me ride and see how safely and well I do it. You can also see Veronica. Her horse is beautiful, but . . ." She let the thought hang in the air, knowing her mother would jump at the chance to compare Prancer to Garnet. It worked.

"Will Mrs. diAngelo be there, too?" Mrs. Atwood asked.

"Probably, Mom, but I don't really know," Lisa said. "See, the car usually picks Veronica up, but it's got tinted windows, and I can't see if Veronica's mother is inside or if it's the chauffeur."

"Really . . . ," Mrs. Atwood said.

Lisa had a feeling that her mother was wondering if they could get the windows on their Ford tinted before tomorrow. But Lisa knew that it didn't matter, even if she was thinking that. What was important was that her mother was going to watch her ride, and that once Mrs. Atwood saw how beautiful Prancer was—how much *more* beautiful she was than Garnet—her signature would be on the permission form in a flash. Lisa knew that as surely as she'd ever known anything about her mother.

Lisa smiled to herself. She'd won.

THE NEXT DAY there was a big note posted in the locker area for Veronica, Lisa, Stevie, and Carole. It was from Max. He wanted to see them all before class.

"It's got to be good news," Stevie said. "I mean, look at the way he signed his name, crossing the *x* with a flourish. He wouldn't do that if he was in a bad mood."

"You are something else," Carole said. "Before, it

was his dimples, and now it's his signature. How do you know when he's in a bad mood or has bad news?"

"Easy," Stevie said immediately. "It's when he calls me Stephanie. Same with my mother. The minute I hear anybody call me that, it's sure to be bad news."

"That doesn't do me any good," Carole said. "My real name is Carole."

"Well, then, I don't see the difference. If somebody called you Stephanie, it would probably be bad news, too."

Carole laughed. Stevie laughed, too. Lisa might have laughed, but her mother was there, watching absolutely everything, and somehow that put a damper on any desire to giggle.

In a few minutes the young riders were ready. The four girls and Mrs. Atwood dutifully filed into Max's office. Max greeted them all, especially Mrs. Atwood, who did not usually come to Lisa's lessons, and asked them to sit down.

"There's one other aspect of Briarwood I wanted to discuss with you four. It's not official from Briarwood's point of view, but it is from mine. As you know, I believe that my riders must all meet certain standards —nothing unreasonable, mere excellence. . . ."

The girls smiled a little nervously. They knew that Max was only half joking, and that was one of the reasons they were proud to be his students.

"I believe that excellence comes from within, however. And I also believe that one person's excellence cannot be judged by another person's standards."

49

That sounded odd, because Max's own standards were always very high and were consistently used to judge his students. In class he was the one who was always telling each of them what to do. Stevie was about to point this out to him, but he had more to say.

"So here's what I want you to do. I want each of you to think about what your own goals are for riding, especially for riding at Briarwood. You will each be in five classes, and that means that you should be thinking about your goals for each of those five classes. For instance, in the Fitting and Showing class, one of you may think of her goal as keeping her horse calm. Another may feel that there's progress to be made on hoof cleaning. When you've decided what your personal goal is, you are going to write it down on a piece of paper and put it in an envelope—one for each class. Then you are going to seal the envelopes and give them to me. After the show we'll meet again. I'll return the envelopes to you, and you can open them to remind yourself of what you thought was important before the competition. You then get to grade yourself. I am not going to ask you what your goals were; I'm simply going to ask you if, in your opinion, you met them. I will then give you whatever ribbon you tell me you deserve."

"You mean if I tell you it's straight blue across the board, you'll give me blue ribbons?" Stevie asked.

"The purpose here is to learn, Stevie," Max said. "If you have learned, you have succeeded."

"And how are you going to break the ties if these

other girls think they've won blue ribbons at the same time I have?" Veronica asked.

Lisa noticed the way Veronica phrased the question. She made it sound as if she, Veronica, would be winning blue ribbons while The Saddle Club girls would only *think* they had. Max noticed it, too.

"Whatever anybody *thinks* is what they are going to get, Veronica," he said patiently. "Now, all of you, go get ready for class. Think about what I've said and think about your personal goals. We'll have a special session to practice for the show after class today. Can everybody stay?"

Stevie, Lisa, and Carole all nodded. Veronica mumbled something about having to reach her mother on the mobile phone. The Saddle Club wasn't interested in her excuses. There was plenty of work to do before class. They dashed for the tack room.

Lisa's mind was in a haze while she tacked up Prancer. All she could think of was how wonderful Briarwood was going to be and how she and Prancer were going to do so well. She thought about what her goals were going to be. There were hundreds of things, she realized. She still sometimes had trouble keeping her legs perpendicular to the ground and her heels down. Sometimes her hands slipped on the reins and gave too much slack. Occasionally she lost track of which diagonal she was supposed to be posting on, and she still wasn't always sure she got her horse to jump at the right distance from the jump. She thought about these things, but she also thought about the horse she was tacking up. Prancer. The horse's name alone was enough to make her dream of blue ribbons. After all, it was the name of one of Santa Claus's reindeer, and it was a good name, because this horse could really fly! She could even soar. And that made Lisa's thoughts soar. With Prancer on her side, she was going to win. There just wasn't any doubt about it.

"That's a pretty horse," her mother remarked, bringing Lisa back to the present.

"She's the greatest," Lisa agreed. "I'll give her a careful grooming after I ride her today, Mom, and if you want to wait around, you'll see how gorgeous she is when her coat is sleek and clean, but even now you can see what a champ she is."

"I guess I can," Mrs. Atwood said. She stepped back a little, though, because Prancer was shifting back and forth uneasily. The mare was much more comfortable and relaxed around young riders than adults, and Mrs. Atwood seemed to be making her a little nervous.

"She won't hurt you, Mom," Lisa promised. "She's just trying to figure out if she trusts you."

"Maybe, but I'm more interested in whether or not she trusts you," Mrs. Atwood said. "Which horse is Veronica diAngelo's?"

"Two stalls down," Lisa said. "Her name is Garnet."

"But that's not Veronica who's putting on her saddle and bridle, is it?" Lisa's mother asked.

"No. Veronica usually gets somebody else to do the work for her." She stood on tiptoe to see who Veronica's victims were this time. They were two younger

girls in the class who were apparently trying to ingrati-
ate themselves with Veronica. They weren't doing a
very good job of it, since they had Garnet's saddle way
too far back on her. That would have to be readjusted
during class, and it wouldn't make Max happy.

Mrs. Atwood stepped away from where Lisa was
working on Prancer and walked over to Garnet's stall.

A few minutes later she reappeared. "Nice horse
Veronica has," she said to Lisa.

"Yes. Garnet's pretty."

"But she's kind of small—I mean, compared to
Prancer, here, isn't she?"

Lisa would never understand what her mother
thought was important, but if the height of a horse
was it, she'd go along with it.

"Arabians aren't known for their height," Lisa said.
"They're known for their endurance and their beautiful heads."

"I think Prancer is really pretty."

"She is," Lisa agreed, recognizing progress when she
heard it. "She's one of the prettiest horses I've ever
known."

"You know, I only care about what's right for you,"
Mrs. Atwood went on.

"Yes, I know," Lisa said. It was true, too. Her
mother sometimes had a skewed notion about what
was desirable, but her intentions were always good.

"I just don't want you to get hurt or anything."

"I won't, Mom. I promise."

"All right. I'll tell Max it's okay."

"You'll sign the form?"

"Yes, I'll sign the form," Mrs. Atwood said. "As a matter of fact, I'll go to Max's office right now and do it."

Lisa wasn't absolutely sure her mother was beyond hearing when she shrieked with joy. It didn't matter, though. All that mattered was she'd be in the ring at Briarwood, and she and Prancer would . . . Could she say it? Yes. They'd win. She just knew it!

6

"AND YOU ALL have to keep an even pace," Max said. "It's extremely important. You can't have your horses dashing around the show ring in spurts. That goes for all the classes, but especially for the jump—Lisa, did you hear me?"

Lisa tugged at Prancer's reins. The mare seemed to think this was a race and she wanted to win. She went faster with every step.

"I heard you," Lisa said. "I'm just not sure Prancer did."

There was nervous laughter.

"You'd better come to a halt now and then start again," Max said.

It took another ten steps before Prancer got Lisa's message about stopping. Lisa decided that poor

Prancer had been cooped up in her stall for over six months, and all she wanted to do now was move, fast. Lisa was sympathetic with that, but she also knew it was her job to be in charge all the time.

"I'm ready to try to canter again," she said.

"And we're waiting for you to do it," Max said. There was an edge to his voice. Lisa knew he was a little annoyed.

"Come on, girl," she whispered to Prancer. "Let's show them how good you can be."

Stevie, Carole, and Veronica had all stopped their horses to give Lisa a chance and to help Prancer concentrate. Lisa nudged Prancer with her legs, shifted her weight, and loosened the reins. Prancer began moving immediately. And as soon as Lisa signaled for a trot, the horse began cantering. A puzzled look crossed Max's face. Then he erased that puzzlement and showed nothing. Prancer was cantering and he was at an even gait. That was, after all, what Max had wanted.

"Nice going," he said.

Lisa beamed. None of the other horses or riders moved until Lisa and Prancer had circled the ring several times. They wanted her to be able to establish a pace that was comfortable for Prancer. It seemed to work.

"All right, now the rest of you please canter."

This time it was Veronica who was having trouble. Her stirrups were too long, and she was having trouble maintaining her balance with her legs extended so far.

It was typical of Veronica that she'd let a small problem like stirrup length interfere with her riding just because readjusting the stirrups involved a little bit of effort. Naturally, she didn't feel she could solve the problem herself. She just *had* to get Max to do it for her.

While Carole, Stevie, and Lisa continued cantering, Max gave his full attention to Veronica's stirrups.

Stevie found this exercise a breeze. Topside was an extremely well-trained horse. He'd belonged to Dorothy DeSoto and had ridden in many, many horse shows. He automatically maintained an even pace at any gait because he'd been so thoroughly trained to do so. Stevie thought she could be doing this in her sleep.

Carole was having a wonderful time, too. When she'd first gotten Starlight, she'd known that he was a young horse who hadn't finished his training. She'd spent hundreds of hours since his arrival last Christmas working on the basics. It was important to have a horse who responded to your commands, especially if you expected to go far with the horse. Carole definitely expected to go far with Starlight, starting at the Briarwood Horse Show.

The only problem Carole was having, in fact, was with Lisa. Every time she looked at Lisa, she grew more concerned. It was bad enough that Lisa had trouble with Prancer when they were working on maintaining a smooth gait, but it got a lot worse when they started to practice jumping.

Prancer could jump all right. The problem was, Prancer couldn't wait to strut her stuff. Lisa was asking her to go over some very low jumps, mostly two or two and a half feet high. The height of the jumps wasn't meant to be a challenge to the horses. The jumps were simply part of the exercise of hunter-jumping competition, which showed the judges how a horse could maintain a smooth gait even while jumping.

Prancer, however, was interested in the height of the jumps. Without any signal from Lisa, she took off way too far in front of the two-foot-high jumps. She fairly flew into the air, soaring over the low jump. Lisa was as unprepared for the landing as she had been for the takeoff. She had to grab on to Prancer's mane just to keep from falling off. While Lisa was startled at first, the feeling of flight was simply exhilarating. The fact that her horse wasn't doing just what she ought to be doing seemed insignificant compared to Prancer's incredible strength. Lisa sighed happily after the first jump and couldn't wait until the second.

"Lisa!" Max cried out.

"Isn't she something?" Lisa asked, grinning proudly.

"Well, I think she needs a little bit more work," Max stammered.

"Oh, of course she needs more work, but she's so wonderful! All her great qualities are going to come out in competition, don't you think?"

Max waited a few minutes before answering the question. "Maybe," he said finally. "Just maybe."

Carole and Stevie exchanged glances. They

couldn't believe how oblivious Lisa was to Prancer's need for more training.

During the next half hour, Max took the group through the rest of the skills he thought they would need to work on before going to Briarwood. Since all of his riders had extensive training in grooming, he wasn't at all concerned about the Fitting and Showing class. He was, however, a little worried about Equitation and spent most of his time working on that.

Lisa listened to everything he said, and she tried to do everything he told her. With every word, though, she was convinced that the reason he was giving her more advice than he was giving her friends was that he believed Prancer was going to win, and he wanted the others to know how hard she had worked for it.

Lisa was still on cloud nine when she took Prancer back to her stall for her final grooming of the day. It was also Lisa's final chance to practice grooming for the show. She wanted to make her horse look perfect.

Stevie finished grooming Topside before her friends were done. She went to Starlight's stall to give Carole a hand with Starlight—and to talk.

"We've got to do something," she said.

Carole didn't need to ask what she was talking about. The problem was Prancer. She was a wonderful horse, but she wasn't ready for a horse show and Lisa seemed totally unaware of her shortcomings.

"We certainly have to try," Carole agreed. "But what can we do?"

"Talk," Stevie said. "We're going to talk to Lisa now."

Carole was willing to go along with that. Together they finished their work on Starlight. Then Stevie and Carole went to find Lisa.

The threesome met up in the hallway of the stable where Prancer was cross-tied. Stevie and Carole each picked up a grooming tool to give Lisa a hand and so they could talk without Mrs. Reg complaining that they weren't working.

"Isn't she beautiful?" Lisa asked.

Stevie and Carole couldn't argue with that.

"She is, definitely," Carole said. "And she's got the makings of a great competition horse." Carole was approaching her topic gingerly. She suspected that Lisa wasn't going to be very receptive.

"In exactly one week," Lisa said, confirming Carole's suspicions.

"Yes, well, that's when Briarwood is, all right," Stevie said. "It's going to be a tough show, you know. A lot of the riders there have been practicing for it for months. Most of them will have had plenty of other show experience, too. We're unusual that way, you know. I mean, you and me. Carole's been in shows before."

"But not like this one," Carole said. "Being in a small show in a small town—well, it's not the same thing as Briarwood."

A dreamy look came over Lisa's face. It made Carole and Stevie nervous. It meant she wasn't listening at all.

"Max said your mother did sign the permission form," Carole said.

"Oh, sure. One look at Prancer and she knew just how I felt. She's really a good person. She misses the point sometimes, but at least she came to the right conclusion—finally. It was a lot of work, I'll tell you. I had to do some serious convincing. I was almost as good as you would have been, Stevie!"

Stevie laughed. "I'm always glad when the good stuff rubs off!" she teased.

"Speaking of good stuff, how about Max's idea for putting our personal goals for Briarwood in sealed envelopes?" Lisa asked.

"I think it's great," Stevie said. "Only problem is, it means thinking. And thinking takes work. Work means time away from focusing on Briarwood and day-dreaming about how exciting it's going to be."

"That's totally illogical," Carole told her. "The more time you spend thinking about how you're going to make it wonderful, the more wonderful it's going to be."

"You're right, of course. But I still think it's a lot of work. I just hope it pays off."

"It will," Carole said. "I promise you. Have you decided what your goals are going to be yet?"

Stevie dropped a brush in Prancer's grooming bucket and picked up the mane comb. She tugged at the mare's mane thoughtfully. "Not yet," she said. "See, first I have to work at it. How about you?"

"I've been working at it," Carole said. She was rubbing Prancer's coat until it gleamed. It was a very satisfying task since the results were so nice. "In a way, though, my goals for the show are going to be a lot of the same goals I've had for Starlight ever since he became mine. He needed so much additional training, and I've given it to him. Now it's paying off. I know there's a lot more work to do. A horse's training can go on for all of his active riding life. I just need to be sure that I use all the skills I have to bring out the best in my horse."

"Oh, Carole, you put it so well!" Lisa said.

When Stevie gave Carole a dirty look, Carole realized that Lisa was still blaming herself for all of Prancer's failings. She tried to adjust what she'd said.

"I mean, that's what's true for me and for my horse. It's not true for everybody. I mean, in the case of a horse who is completely new to pleasure riding and competition, it might be a totally different story. . . ."

"For some horses, maybe," Lisa said. "But you've really given me something to think about." She punctuated that sentence by dropping the brush she'd been using into the grooming bucket. "There. I'm done," she announced. She unclipped Prancer from her crossties and led her to her stall. She checked that there was fresh hay and water and then latched the door behind her.

"I think I'd better get the envelope and the paper from Max and hurry on home," Lisa said. "Sorry to dash off, but I've got some homework to do. I'll talk to you guys this week, a lot, okay?"

"Okay," Stevie said. "Good luck with the work you have to do."

"Thanks. Bye." And then she was gone.

"What was that all about?" Stevie asked.

"It's about trouble," Carole said. Stevie certainly agreed with her on that.

"What do you think she's going to put down for her goals?"

Carole shook her head. "I don't know, but unless a miracle happens in the next seven days, I know what her goal *ought* to be."

"What's that?"

"*Staying* on Prancer through five classes."

Considering what they'd seen in practice, Stevie had to agree.

7

STEVIE STARED AT the five blank pieces of paper in front of her. Homework was just about her least favorite thing in the whole world, and it seemed to her that what Max had asked his riders to do was homework. Still, it was also horsework, and anything to do with horses couldn't be all bad.

To start with, she wrote the names of the five classes she'd be entering at the top of each of the pieces of paper: Fitting and Showing, Equitation, Pleasure, Trail, and Jumping.

She growled. That hadn't inspired her at all. She picked up her pencil again and began chewing on the eraser. She had never understood why having little pieces of rubber in your mouth was supposed to help you think. She stopped chewing on the eraser and tried thinking about horses and horse shows. That seemed to help.

Fitting and Showing was basically a test of grooming skills. She was good at that. She was about the best in the stable at using a hoof pick, so that couldn't be a goal. She sometimes got lazy when it came to getting all the tangles out of Topside's mane. She jotted that down. "Four to go," she told the wall of her room.

In Equitation, it seemed to her that Topside was so well trained, he was going to do most of the work. Still, if it looked as if she weren't doing anything, she wouldn't place. She knew that. In a way, the important thing in that class was going to be keeping up with Topside. That meant making her own movements as smooth and seamless as his. It also meant that she'd have a special opportunity to pay more attention to herself than to her horse. She wanted to work on the position of her hands and being sure that her legs remained supple while she gave Topside nearly invisible aids. She'd had trouble with that in the past, and she hoped she'd be able to do it right this time. She wrote that down. "Three to go." She turned her attention to the paper marked "Pleasure."

Carole made a face at the computer screen as she read the message that Cam had left for her.

> . . . *I can't believe I'm actually going to meet you at Briarwood! It seems like we've been writing*

notes about horses for such a long time. Now we'll get to talk instead of write. Isn't that great?

"No," Carole mumbled. Talking with Cam probably wouldn't be any more fun than writing to her. The note went on:

> We had class today. I'm sure you did, too, since I recall that you have class every Saturday. We won't mind missing it next week, though, will we? Anyway, today Mr. Barclay was drilling us on show techniques. He says the judges look out for these incredibly small things—like if your tie is straight or if there's a smudge on your boots. He's going to have an inspection before the show starts, and if I know him, he'll have extra shoe polish with him. He also drilled us on riding techniques. For the jumping, he had us going over phantom jumps. There were cavalletti poles on the ground, and he wanted us to get our horses to jump them as if they were three feet high. He said that would help us know how to tell our horses how high to jump regardless of the height of the jump. It was hard, but I think I understand the technique. It has to do with controlling your horse, and that's very important at a horse show.

Carole certainly agreed with that. She wondered why it was that Max hadn't had her class working that way with cavalletti. A wave of uncertainty washed over her. She'd always been convinced that Max Regnery was the best teacher in the world. What if Mr. Barclay was better? What if Cam was a better rider?

"Whoa, girl," she told herself. Max *was* the best teacher in the world. Carole had always believed that. Why should she stop believing it now? Had Cam's precious Mr. Barclay come up with the wonderful idea of personal goals? Carole didn't think so. She'd show Cam how wonderful Max was.

She tapped at the keys of her computer and brought up a fresh screen.

> *Hi, Cam! I'm back from class. We were working hard on our skills, too, but not over cavalletti the way you described. That must have been hard work.*

Carole meant it when she wrote it—she just wasn't convinced that the drills would be all that helpful in preparing for the competition. She continued.

> *Max came up with something really good. He's making us all think about what our personal goals are for the show and then write them down. We're going to put them into sealed envelopes and open them after the show, just to remind ourselves of what we thought was important for us to learn. And then we get to decide whether we met our goals or not. Isn't that great? Max is so smart!*

She sent the message, then turned off her computer, and focused her attention on the five small sheets of paper and the envelope in front of her. She picked up her pen. It was a special pen. It was a pen she'd bought when she and her friends had been in New York, staying with Dorothy DeSoto when Dorothy was competing in the American Horse Show. Since it was connected with all those horsey things, Carole had a weird feeling that it had some special power, even though it was just a tourist's pen with a picture of the Empire State Building on one side and the Statue of Liberty on the other. Every time Carole looked at it, all she could think of was horses.

She picked up one sheet of paper and wrote "Jumping" at the top of it. Starlight was a naturally wonderful jumper, though he tended to prefer the excitement of jumping high to the structure of proper hunter jumping, where style was the important part. Carole wondered briefly whether Starlight might not have benefited from working with cavalletti the way Cam had. Then she dismissed the thought. If Max had thought that would be good for her, he would have had her do it. Wouldn't he?

Carole tried to focus on what was important for her and for Starlight in the Jumping class. Beating Cam. That's what came into her head, and it was hard to dismiss. She wanted to beat Cam. She wanted to be better than Cam. She wanted Max to be a better teacher than Mr. Barclay. She didn't care if she got a blue. She just wanted to get a higher ribbon than Cam's.

This is all wrong, she told herself. Horse shows were about being the best rider you could be for yourself. That was why Max had them write down their goals. It didn't matter how good, or bad, the other riders were. It only mattered that you did your best. If everybody else in the class was really terrible, a blue ribbon didn't mean anything unless you thought you'd done a good job. Carole reminded herself of these things and began the job of thinking about her goals all over again.

"Keep an even pace and don't let Starlight jump too high over the low jumps," she wrote.

She reread her own words and nodded. Yes, she thought, that was a worthwhile goal—and not an easy one, either, on a horse who sometimes thought he was an eagle.

She reached for her next piece of paper.

LISA WASN'T CONVINCED that Max's idea about personal goals was really a good one. Wasn't that the reason why there were judges at horse shows? The idea seemed to be that a horse show was an opportunity to compete against other riders of approximately the same skill level and let somebody else decide who was actually the best.

It didn't really matter, though, what Lisa thought about writing down her personal goals. Max wanted them to do it, so it had to be done.

Lisa put on her pajamas, then grabbed pen and paper, and settled comfortably in bed.

She closed her eyes and forced herself to think about everything she'd learned about horseback riding from the first time she had been on a horse. It was all there—in her mind. She remembered when getting into a saddle seemed like an awkward and difficult task. Now it felt like the most natural motion in the world. At first the horses' gaits had seemed odd, unfamiliar. Now her own body responded automatically to the movements of the horses at every gait. The first time she'd jumped, she had been amazed to find herself still on her horse after the horse landed. Now she always knew she'd be there. She was a rider. She was a good rider. And she had the best horse in the world.

Her mind also filled with recollections of all the riding she'd done, mostly with Stevie and Carole. The recollections were wonderful ones, filled with joy and excitement, peace and contentment. The thoughts carried her into sleep.

Lisa could feel the smooth, supple movement of Prancer beneath her. The mare's coat gleamed in the bright sunshine. As Prancer shook her head, her inky mane caught the light, and then lay smooth and shiny once again. Her saddle had a rich luster—one that came only from the best and most thorough cleaning.

"Lisa Atwood on Prancer," the public-address system blared. That was it. It was her signal. She was ready. But for what? Lisa looked about her quickly. The ring was filled with obstacles, about three feet

70

high. This was the jump competition, and she had no idea what the path was! She was filled with terror and panic. Then, without a signal from her, Prancer entered the ring. The horse looked around the ring, nodded as if to tell Lisa she knew what she was doing and there was nothing for Lisa to worry about. Lisa knew, as certainly as she'd ever known anything in her life, that she was going to be fine. She gave Prancer a little nudge with her legs, and they were off.

Without hesitation Prancer broke into a smooth canter, aimed herself toward the first jump at an even gait, and began the work she'd been born to do so well. Three feet from the first jump, Lisa leaned forward, rose up ever so slightly, gave Prancer the rein she needed to do her job. The pair flew over the jump, landing so smoothly Lisa barely realized they were on the ground. There was scattered applause from the audience. Prancer's whole body curved to turn gracefully toward the next jump. She changed her lead naturally and approached the next jump with the same confidence she'd used on the first. Lisa prepared for the jump, and again the two of them went over easily. Lisa was aware that Prancer's tail rose with the jump so that it flowed after them, like the tail of a comet. When they landed this time, there was more applause.

The course had ten jumps in it, and every one was as easy as the first. Prancer navigated the complicated trail as if she'd jumped it a thousand times before. Lisa stayed in the saddle, focusing on her own form, head up, eyes forward, legs in, heels down, hands firm but not tight, lower arms parallel to the ground, lower legs at right angles to the ground. . . . The list was endless, and she'd heard it a thousand times. Sometimes it seemed as if she heard it a thousand times each class. For once, however, she didn't hear it from Max or her friends. She heard it from herself, and she was just checking that she was doing it all right. She was. It was the easiest, most natural feeling she'd ever had. She was riding, and she was riding well. Prancer was making it right for her.

The tenth jump was up ahead. Again they soared. Again the audience clapped. This time very loudly.

The course was done. Prancer drew to a halt in front of the judges' stand and stood motionless while the judges tallied their scores. The judge in the center stood up.

"Ladies and gentlemen," she said. "There is no point in continuing this competition. This rider, Miss Lisa Atwood, is simply the finest rider any of us has ever seen. And her horse, Prancer, defies all description. This may be just a local horse show, but you have been treated here to a performance that could take the blue even at the American Horse Show. We don't need to see any other riders, we have our winner right here!"

The audience applauded loudly.

"Miss Atwood, Prancer, please come forward," the judge said.

Lisa could barely believe what was happening, but she knew, as she'd never known anything before, that she deserved it. She and Prancer had been the best—the very best—that the judges had ever seen. She signaled Prancer to step forward to where a small red carpet had been rolled out.

The three judges approached her. The main judge held the blue ribbon for the Jumping class.

She reached up and clipped it onto Prancer's bridle. The gesture seemed somehow familiar. Then Lisa recalled that this wasn't the first time she'd received a blue ribbon that day. She and Prancer had already taken blues in all her other classes, too!

There was just one prize left. Would it be hers? She just had to know.

She leaned forward in her saddle to speak to the judge. The judge looked back up at her, filled with awe.

Lisa drew on her courage.

"Does this mean that I'm . . . ?"

The judge smiled and spoke the word Lisa had been unable to utter. "Champion," she said. "Yes, you are the champion!"

It was all so much, so fast, and so wonderful! She could barely believe it, and it was hard to think about, too, because the whole audience was standing and applauding and shouting. Waves of noise, loud sounds, filled Lisa's ears and her whole head. They didn't stop. They persisted and persisted. The applause and the shouts merged into an overwhelming . . .

Buzzzzzzz.

It was Lisa's alarm clock.

She awoke with a start, brought back to reality with the unpleasant noise that still couldn't erase the wonderful feeling she had just thinking back on her dream.

Lisa found that she was still clutching five pieces of white paper in her hand. Her dream had been wonderful and exciting, but it had been something more, too. It had told her what her personal goal was for Briarwood.

She picked up the pencil that was still on her bed and wrote the same word five times: "Blue."

She put the papers in an envelope, licked it, and sealed it. She stood up and headed for the bathroom, uttering the word from her dream that was still with her: "Champion."

She liked the sound of that.

CAROLE WAS SURROUNDED by her friends. Lisa was working on Prancer in the stall on one side of her. Stevie and Topside were on the other side. They were all grooming their horses in the temporary stalls that Briarwood had erected for the competitors. All the Juniors were in the same area. Fortunately for The Saddle Club, Veronica and Garnet had been assigned a stall two aisles away.

Carole glanced at Lisa. She was working very hard on Prancer's grooming. The mare seemed to love the attention—as she always did—and the results were great. Prancer certainly was a beautiful horse, and her fine bloodlines showed to their best advantage with a good grooming.

On her other side, Stevie was also working hard.

She chatted on and on with Topside as she groomed him. Carole tried not to listen, but it wasn't easy.

"So the trick today, Topside, is going to be making it look as if I'm doing some of the work and not you. I know this stuff is all old hat—or should I say old bridle, since you're a horse?—to you, but it's new to me, and I'm pretty nervous. I can tell you are as cool as a cucumber. Well I'm not. . . ."

Carole decided that anything Topside could say to put Stevie at ease would be more comforting than anything Carole might say, especially since Carole herself was nervous. She wondered briefly if Topside might have any words of comfort for her. Then she realized it wasn't words of comfort she needed, but her dandy brush, which she must have left in the van.

She gave Starlight a gentle pat on his rear to move him over and allow her out of the stall. He obliged. She slipped out, fastening the door behind her. She asked both Lisa and Stevie if they needed anything from the van. Both just shook their heads. They were concentrating very hard on grooming their horses. Yes, Carole thought. It is nice being surrounded by friends—even if they don't know you're there.

There were a lot of young riders. Carole saw quite a few that looked like beginners who wouldn't be competing in her class, but she also saw more than ten others who probably were competitors. Then Carole remembered that one of them was Cam Nelson. But which one?

One girl was struggling to groom an ugly little pony.

Carole knew that what a horse looked like really didn't matter, but all the grooming in the world wasn't going to make that ugly pony a winner. Still, she didn't think the girl was Cam. The pony was a mare and Cam's horse was a gelding. Then Carole noticed that the girl had put her horse's name plaque on the door of the stall. "Grumpy," it said. Definitely not Cam.

Then Carole spotted another girl who might be Cam. She had long braids, and her horse was a gelding. No, it couldn't be Cam. She was just too young to be Cam Nelson.

Carole decided this wasn't really a good time to be looking for Cam. She'd meet her soon enough, and her real job here was collecting her dandy brush and finishing Starlight's grooming.

She picked up her pace and headed for the lot where the van was parked. It took her only a minute to find the dandy brush. It was exactly where she thought she'd left it. At least something was going right. She hurried back to Starlight.

She got delayed, however, because there was a boy who was bringing his horse out of the stall for a stretch and a walk. The boy was about her age. He was tall with nice features. He had black hair, deep brown eyes, and light brown skin. The fact that he was a good-looking boy wasn't what she noticed first about him, though. It was his horse that got her attention. The horse, a gleaming chestnut, was just beautiful! He was sleek and elegant and perfectly groomed.

"Nice horse!" she said to the boy in honest admiration. She also made a mental note to herself to be sure to do as good a job on Starlight's grooming.

"Good old Duffy always looks great for a show. He just loves them," the boy said.

"Duffy?" Carole said. That was Cam's horse's name! What a coincidence. "There's a girl here with a horse by the same name!" she said.

"Really? How funny," the boy said. "Who is it?"

"Her name is Cam Nelson," Carole said.

The boy smiled. "That's funny, too, because *my* name is Cam Nelson."

"Cam?"

"Carole?"

She nodded automatically in response, but her mind was racing. A *boy*? How could that be, Carole wondered. She and a *girl* named Cam had been furiously writing notes back and forth, and now Carole had discovered that Cam wasn't a girl at all. How could she have been so wrong?

Actually, she told herself, what difference did it make? The whole situation was pretty funny. She laughed aloud and offered him her hand.

"Glad to meet you, finally," she said.

He shook it. "Me, too," he told her.

"Uh, sorry about the girl thing," she said. "I just thought Cam was, uh, a girl's name."

"It is, sometimes," he said. "But not in my case. I'm really Cameron."

"And I'm really Carole," she countered.

They both smiled at her joke. Carole was going to say something else when the public-address system clicked on.

"The Intermediate Fitting and Showing class will commence in thirty minutes," the voice announced. "All entrants must be in the East ring in twenty-five minutes."

That meant that Carole had approximately twenty-three minutes to finish Starlight's grooming *and* her own. There was work to be done.

"See you later!" she called.

"You can count on it!" Cam said after her.

Carole liked the sound of that.

LISA WAS SURE that everything was perfect. There was no doubt in her mind that Prancer was going to be the most beautiful and best groomed horse in the ring. She also knew that, thanks to her mother's ministrations, her own grooming was just fine. Once her mother had decided that she should be in the horse show, she'd decided she was going to do it right. Her clothes had been specially fitted by a tailor, and she looked great. That was what this event was about. She even had new boots to replace the ones that had been pinching her toes.

Lisa and Prancer were standing in the East ring with all the other riders in the class, waiting to be told to go into the show ring. This wasn't a riding class. The horses didn't have their saddles on, just their bridles. This class was meant to show the judges that the riders knew how to prepare their horses for the classes to come and to demonstrate grooming and the fact that the horses were in good physical condition. One look at Prancer and anybody would know she was in great condition.

Nearby, Carole was all business, rubbing Starlight's coat one more time with a handkerchief that a boy with a chestnut horse had loaned to her. She finished the wipe and handed the handkerchief back to the boy with a nod of thanks. Stevie and Topside stood next to Carole. Both Stevie and her horse seemed very relaxed. Lisa remembered that Topside had spent many years at horse shows before he'd come to Pine Hollow. He simply exuded confidence. Confidence was important. Lisa knew that. But it wasn't everything.

Then there was Veronica. As usual, Veronica and her horse looked great. Lisa was sure, however, that the judges wouldn't be fooled by the fact that Garnet was simply not as fine a horse as Prancer.

Prancer shifted her weight and lifted her front feet nervously, first her right, then her left. She seemed uneasy and crowded by all the other horses. Lisa patted her neck to put her at ease. The horse nodded her head and then shook it, mussing her mane. Lisa smoothed it.

"This way, riders!" a woman announced, calling everybody in the ring to the gate that led to the show ring.

With those words everything in the world faded to

gray for Lisa—everything, that was, except for herself, her horse, and the judges. She held Prancer's reins firmly and followed the horse in front of her into the ring, to her fate, to her certain blue ribbon.

The horses and riders were asked to line up in front of the judges' stand. Like an automaton, Lisa followed the directions. She and Prancer stood between the boy who had given his handkerchief to Carole and a girl she'd never seen before.

Lisa stood at attention, facing straight forward. She clutched Prancer's reins, only vaguely aware that the mare kept tugging at them.

There was activity all around Lisa and Prancer, and Lisa saw almost none of it. Judges circled the horses, checking both grooming and conformation, making notes, asking questions.

"Uh-oh, here comes the judge!" the boy next to Lisa joked. She didn't think it was funny. She stood at attention, eyes straight forward.

"Relax," the boy said to her. "They're looking at your horse's conformation, not your posture."

She really didn't think that was funny at all. But then, though he had a nice chestnut horse, whom he called Duffy, the horse wasn't anything special, and he didn't have a chance at a ribbon. Maybe he was even trying to distract her so he could get a blue instead of her. No way, she thought, quickly returning her attention to her own quest for blue. Eyes forward, she gripped the reins. Her knuckles were white.

Lisa felt Prancer tug hard at the reins. She didn't

dare turn around. She was sure that the slightest movement on her part would be an error and cost her a ribbon.

"Hi there," the judge said to Lisa.

Lisa's eyes flicked toward the woman. "Hello, ma'am," Lisa said in a military response.

"Your horse seems uneasy," the judge commented.

"She's fine," Lisa assured the judge.

"I don't know about that. She keeps shifting around. She's as nervous as you are."

"Oh, I'm not nervous," Lisa said. It was true. She wasn't nervous. She was doing everything exactly the way she thought she ought to. She was going to get a blue ribbon.

"Well, I'm going to check out the mare's conformation. Hold her steady, okay?"

"Yes, ma'am," Lisa said. She wrapped the reins around her hand more tightly, completely forgetting how dangerous that could be if the horse took off. She could hurt her arm badly that way.

Lisa didn't dare watch while the judge examined Prancer, but then she didn't need to, either. She was confident that Prancer was the best, most beautiful horse in the ring. If she watched the judge do the examination, it might suggest that she wasn't confident. She continued to look straight ahead.

If Lisa was confident, Prancer didn't seem to be. The horse almost jumped back from the judge. That was when Lisa remembered that Prancer really liked kids and didn't seem to like adults much. The judge was definitely an adult, and Prancer was trying to move away from her.

Lisa didn't see what happened next. Later people told her about it, though.

The judge ran her hand along Prancer's flank and then down the mare's leg. It was more than the over-excited horse could take. She bucked. She simply lifted her hind quarters off the ground and kicked back. It wouldn't have been so bad if the judge hadn't been crouched there, checking out her hind legs at the time. Prancer wound up kicking the judge in the rib cage.

"Yeouch!" the woman howled.

Lisa looked around then and saw that half the people were looking at the judge in concern. The other half were scowling at Lisa! Lisa's jaw dropped in astonishment.

Another of the judges came running over to help the woman off the ground.

"Move the horse!" he said sternly to Lisa. That was when Lisa realized what had happened. Her horse, her precious Prancer, had actually knocked the judge onto the ground. The other judge was afraid she was going to do it again, too!

"I'm sorry," Lisa said.

The man looked at her. "You're excused," he said.

She was surprised he accepted her apology so easily. "Can I do something?" she offered.

"You can leave the ring," he said.

Leave the ring? Suddenly Lisa realized that "You're

excused" didn't mean he'd accepted her apology. It meant she was excused from the class. She'd flunked. She was out. Done. No blue. No ribbon at all. Just gone.

And if any doubt remained in her mind, what came over the public-address system cleared it up completely.

"Competitor number two seventy-three has been disqualified. Lisa Atwood, please remove your horse from the ring."

Lisa didn't see the looks on her friends' faces. She didn't hear Carole whisper, "Talk to you later," or Stevie's "Tough luck!" All she was aware of was her own humiliation and her own broken dream. She'd been disqualified. The horse show was over for her and for Prancer.

LISA'S FEET MARCHED and her mind raced as she led Prancer out of the show ring. She saw only the dark interior of the stabling area ahead, and she never felt the annoyed tugging on the lead rope. The only thing in her mind was anger.

This time it wasn't my fault, she thought. Prancer is far and away the finest horse in the ring. The only way Prancer would have bucked and kicked the judge would be if the judge provoked her.

That was it, then, Lisa was sure. It had to be the answer. She decided the judge must have somehow resented the fact that an Intermediate rider had such a fine and valuable horse and had found a way to get her out of the competition. Maybe it was because the judge had always wished *she* could have ridden a horse like Prancer. Or maybe somebody she'd known when she was a kid did have a horse like Prancer and she was jealous. Or maybe the judge actually didn't like young riders and wanted to be mean. Or maybe—

"I knew another young rider who had that happen once," a voice said to Lisa. She looked up. It was Mrs. Reg. She was standing by Prancer's stall. Lisa realized with a little surprise that she'd apparently been waiting for Lisa and Prancer there.

Lisa didn't say anything. There wasn't any point in it. Some days there wasn't any point in anything at all.

Mrs. Reg didn't seem to notice that Lisa hadn't answered. She went on talking.

"He was a fine young rider with great potential."

Lisa groaned inwardly. Mrs. Reg was well-known for her endless supply of stories. The stories were always about horses; they were always about something that happened a long time ago; and they always related to something that had just happened. Usually, the trick was figuring out exactly how they related to what had just happened.

Right now Lisa wasn't interested in what Mrs. Reg had to say—unless it had to do with a judge who had it in for a rider in a show. That didn't seem to be what this was about.

"So this young boy fell for a new horse that came to the stable—Lightning was his name, I think. The boy was bound and determined to take him out on a trail ride. Max—*my* Max, that is—" She meant, then, that

86

it was her husband Max, not the current Max, who was her son. "Max told the boy the horse wasn't ready. He hadn't finished his training. The boy said the horse had all the training he needed to go out on the trail. In a way, he was right. The horse knew what he was doing. Didn't need the boy to tell him anything. As a result, he didn't listen to anything the boy told him."

Mrs. Reg stopped talking. Lisa was annoyed because the story didn't have anything to do with a judge, but her curiosity was piqued. She couldn't help herself. She asked the question.

"So what happened?"

Mrs. Reg looked confused, as if the story was totally self-explanatory and no question should have been asked. Then she shrugged her shoulders and continued, briefly. "Oh, the boy got out of the hospital in a week or so. He's fine now."

That was it. Mrs. Reg's story was finished, and she wasn't going to say anything more. She held the stall door for Lisa and Prancer. Once the horse was inside and Lisa was out, Mrs. Reg closed the door and fastened the latch. She walked off, muttering something about saddle soap, leaving Lisa to herself.

Lisa was by herself. In fact, she felt as alone as she could ever remember feeling. All her dreams had been shattered in one quick kick and a simple word from a judge. "Disqualified." Now it seemed that it was going to get even worse. She couldn't leave. Her mother and father were coming, but not until the afternoon, and she couldn't even reach them to have them come get her now. She had to stay. But she didn't have to stay where anybody could see her or talk to her or try to comfort her or tell her dumb stories about riders who ended up in the hospital. She decided that she wanted to be as much by herself as she felt.

She looked around the temporary stalls and didn't see anyplace to go. She wandered into Briarwood's stables and found what she was looking for—a staircase. She climbed up to the stable's loft. It was just what she wanted: empty.

It was empty of people anyway. There were only bales of hay, sweet-smelling, fresh hay. No horses, no kids, and best of all, no judges. She sat on one bale and leaned on another.

Around her and below, she could hear the horse show continuing relentlessly without her. The crowd buzzed with excited interest. Here and there horses whinnied and stomped. She could smell the rich, warm aroma of horses. But she wasn't part of it. She was in the loft, above it all, separated, alone—very much alone.

She tried to shut out the sounds of the show beneath her, but they wouldn't go. The amplifier for the public-address system had been mounted just outside the upper door to the loft. The loft was filled with the sound of the judges' instructions, blaring through the microphones.

"Please walk your horses in a circle, clockwise. Now trot. Now, beginning with number eighteen, please change directions at the half circle. Good. Thank you. Now line up again—in order. Thank you."

It was all a blur. One second Lisa felt as though she were still down in the ring with her friends. The next second Lisa felt a million miles away. And though she was actually only a few feet from the competition, she might as well have been a million miles away. *Disqualified.*

The amplifiers were quiet for a few minutes. Curiosity took Lisa to the large window that overlooked the ring. She found she had the best seat in the house. Nobody seemed to notice her, but she could see everything.

Fourteen horses were lined up in the ring, and next to each one stood a rider. They waited patiently. Some of the kids chatted with the other competitors. Others patted their horses. None of them seemed to find it necessary to stand at attention, eyes straight ahead, gripping the rope. Lisa wondered about that. If nobody had really good form, would the judges actually award the blue ribbon to anybody?

Then she looked at the horses. Each was groomed to gleaming perfection. Manes were combed, or in some cases braided. Hooves had been polished a shiny black. They all really looked good. Some of the horses were actually better looking than others, but all of them were fit for showing. Her eyes went to Topside and Starlight. Her friends stood proudly with their horses. They'd each worked hard and deserved credit for the great results. Lisa was glad for her friends that the judge hadn't gone after *their* horses the way she had gone after Prancer. If Lisa couldn't win, at least maybe her friends could. That thought made her feel a little better.

Then the judges came out into the ring with the ribbons. It was time to announce winners.

"The first prize, blue ribbon, goes to Miss Veronica diAngelo and her horse, Garnet."

Veronica?! The judges had to be crazy!

The audience didn't seem to agree with Lisa. There was genuine applause as Veronica stepped forward to collect her ribbon. Garnet followed docilely and seemed pleased to have the ribbon attached to her halter. Veronica positively beamed as she waited for the other ribbons to be awarded.

Life wasn't fair. Lisa had done everything she could to see that she would win the blue ribbon. She had the best horse, she'd done the most work on the horse's grooming. How could it be that somebody as awful and undeserving as Veronica diAngelo would win it?

A strange and unfamiliar feeling came over Lisa. It was jealousy. She'd never had cause to be envious of other riders before. She'd always done well. She'd always succeeded at anything she'd ever tried. She'd never been the one who was left out or forced out. Yet now she was. She was alone, up in the loft, watching her friends do what she wanted to do more than anything in the world, and watching the girl she hated the most get the ribbon Lisa felt she deserved.

The first tear rolled down her cheek, followed quickly by another, and then a flood. It seemed as though they wouldn't stop. Through the blur of her tears, she watched the judges award the rest of the ribbons. Red went to the boy with the horse named Duffy. Yellow went to somebody Lisa had not even noticed. Carole got white and Stevie got pink for fifth place. Lisa stared blankly out of the loft window and the rest of the proceedings. She barely noticed while Veronica proudly walked her horse around the ring and then received what appeared to be genuine congratulations from the other competitors—including Stevie and Carole. None of it seemed to Lisa to make any sense, and none of it made any difference. She and Prancer had been disqualified.

There was a ten-minute break then while the riders tacked up their horses and prepared for the first riding class of the day, Equitation. Lisa didn't move.

She was still sitting there, staring out of the loft window, when the horses reentered the ring, this time under mount.

"Riders, a rising trot please, clockwise," the judge instructed them.

On signal from their riders, the horses began trotting instantly, and, in turn, the riders began posting with the two-beat gait. Lisa's eyes followed Stevie on Topside. Her form seemed almost perfect. Stevie's lower legs remained nearly motionless, while her upper legs easily lifted her ever so slightly out of the saddle. Her forearms remained in a straight line with the reins to Topside's mouth. But her shoulders seemed a little stiff. Stevie should relax them, Lisa told herself. If she were riding, if she were in the ring with Prancer, she'd be able to do it. She'd make it look right. Prancer could do it better than Topside. She was sure. If only . . .

STEVIE RELAXED HER shoulders. She'd been holding them too stiffly, and it wasn't right for a rising trot. It wasn't right for any gait, actually. It was important for a rider to look relaxed. Topside was doing everything right; now Stevie had to do as well as her horse was doing.

"Now change directions at the half school," the judge instructed the riders. She pointed to Stevie, meaning she was supposed to be the first rider to do it. She got a third of the way along the side of the ring, about eight on a clock face, put mild pressure on Topside with her outside leg, moved her inside hand ever so slightly to instruct Topside with the rein, and found the horse doing exactly what she wanted him to do. Halfway across the ring on the diagonal, Stevie sat for two beats of the trot, changing her posting diagonal, and then resumed a normal rising trot.

Perfect, she told herself, and she was right.

She smiled proudly. It wasn't a hard thing to do. She'd done it hundreds of times, only she'd never done it in a show before, in front of a crowd and in front of judges. Her experience told her that often the things that seemed the simplest turned out to be the hardest in a stressful situation. This was certainly stress. She'd known Topside would do the right thing. It was Stevie she'd been worried about. However, she'd come through for herself, and she felt good about it.

"And now canter, beginning at the A," the judge instructed. The ring was marked with the letters of the alphabet for dressage. A was at the center of the far end. The riders had to maintain a trot until they got there, and then they were to begin their canter. Stevie watched while several of the riders' horses burst into a canter well before they reached A. The problem was that the horses had heard the word and followed the oral instruction of the judge instead of the instructions from their riders. That was really bad form. When a few of the horses started cantering, all the rest of them wanted to as well. Horses were naturally competitive animals and always wanted to keep up with, and pass, the horse in front of them. The judges watched keenly.

Topside behaved beautifully. He waited patiently for Stevie to give him his instructions, maintaining an

94

even trot while they circled the ring until point A. Stevie then moved her outside leg behind Topside's girth, touched his belly gently with her foot, and relaxed while he moved into his lilting canter. She noticed the judge nod approval. She kept her own smile to a minimum.

Starlight was having a hard time, and, as a result, so was Carole. Carole had known this would be the most difficult class for Starlight. He was a great horse, but details were not his strong point. From the day she'd gotten Starlight, Carole had been working on his training, knowing that he would have to develop better manners if he was ever going to be a champion. He'd learned an awful lot and was much better than he had been. He wasn't perfect yet, though, and this was hard for him. The minute another horse started cantering, Starlight wanted to canter, too. Carole held him back, but it wasn't easy, and the judges noticed. It was as if she could feel their eyes, missing nothing. They seemed to be even tougher than Max!

Where was Max? Carole looked around, wondering if he was watching. And where was Mrs. Reg? She was sure they were both in the audience, unless . . .

Starlight tugged at the reins. He was ready to go, but Carole wasn't. She turned all her attention to her horse and looked straight ahead, just as she should have been doing when her mind had wandered. She couldn't let her mind wander any more than she could let her eyes wander. Horses seemed to be able to sense a change of balance when a rider's head turned, and they were likely to begin to turn themselves when that happened. It took Carole just a second to get both herself and Starlight back on track. But it was a second that she was sure the judges had noticed. She was determined to do better.

She and Starlight began her canter. As the judges seemed to notice everything that went wrong, Carole hoped they noticed everything that went right. Starlight's canter was the most unbelievably smooth, rocking gait in the world. Carole was sure she could spend her entire life riding Starlight at a canter. She felt the utter joy of it as they rounded the ring together. The smile on her face must have been noticed by a judge, then, because, though she *was* looking straight ahead, she could see the judge smiling back at her.

The judges began giving the riders more instructions. The horses made an S-curve down the center of the ring at a walk, and then at a sitting trot. Carole knew that she and Starlight were doing better than they had at first, but she wasn't sure they were doing well enough. Stevie, on the other hand, was doing beautifully.

Everything was working right for Stevie and Topside. From the very first moment in the ring, Topside had simply done everything Stevie could possibly have asked of him. He was a champion, and he was making her look good. Since Stevie didn't have to worry about her horse, she could focus on herself. She tried to remember everything she had to do, and then she did it. She found herself enjoying every minute of it.

It was coming to an end, though. The judges had the riders bring their horses to a walk and asked them to continue walking while they made their decisions. It didn't take long. There was just no question about who had earned the blue. It was Stevie Lake on Topside.

Even though Stevie had been certain they'd done a great job, she was still surprised when she heard her name called. It was impossible, wasn't it? There were fourteen other riders here, and they were all good, weren't they? Was she really the best?

"Go on!" Carole whispered to her. "You deserve it!"

If Carole said so, it had to be true. Stevie turned Topside over to the judges' stand and watched with pride as the judge clipped the bright blue ribbon onto Topside's bridle.

"Congratulations," the judge said. "Topside is a great horse, and you're a fine rider."

"Thank you," Stevie said, shaking the woman's hand. Then she rode a few feet away and waited while the rest of the ribbons were given out. Carole's friend, Cam, whom Stevie had met between classes, took second place. That seemed fair. He was an awfully good rider, and his horse, Duffy, was very well trained and responsive. Starlight had been giving Carole trouble, and the judges obviously noticed it, because Carole got only fifth place. Veronica got a seventh-place ribbon. Stevie noticed her glaring at it with displeasure just before the judges told Stevie she could take Top-

side off on a victory gallop. It was a wonderful moment. While all the other riders stood still on their
horses out of respect for the blue-ribbon winner,
Stevie turned Topside to her right and let him go. He
swept around the ring joyously, feeling the admiration
of the crowd. Stevie spotted Max and Mrs. Reg in the
front row of the audience. They waved at her proudly.
She nodded politely, deciding it wouldn't be polite to
wave back. It would be like showing off, though the
victory gallop itself was the biggest show-off of all.
Stevie loved every second of it. She drew her horse to
a halt back near the judges and next to Carole, who
offered her hand for a high five. That didn't feel like
showing off. That felt like being congratulated by her
best friend. It was wonderful! And then Stevie got to
lead the class back out of the ring.

Carole was thrilled for Stevie, who definitely had
deserved the blue ribbon in that class, but she was
disappointed for herself. It wasn't so much that she'd
wanted to beat Stevie. She had just wanted Starlight
to do better in Equitation than he'd done. She
scowled at Starlight. Was it really his fault, though?
she asked herself. Training a horse was a long and
arduous task. And now she understood from what had
happened that she had a lot more work to do. She was
pretty sure she could do it. She hoped she could do a
lot of it before Briarwood next year, if she got asked
back.

"What happened?" a voice asked. Carole turned
around and found herself looking at Cam. His concern

98

seemed genuine. "It seemed to me that you and Starlight were doing great, especially when he got to cantering."

"He lost his train of thought," Carole said truthfully. "I guess I did, too. And the judges noticed."

"It's like Murphy's Law," Cam said. "If something can go wrong, it will. At horse shows it works like this: If something goes wrong, even for a split second, that's when the judges will be looking."

Carole smiled and nodded agreement. "Well, for most of the class, Starlight was great—"

"It seemed to me that his rider was as great as he was," Cam interrupted.

"Thanks, but I goofed, too. I just got lax for a few seconds, and by the time I noticed, the judge had noticed. I have to find a way to keep Starlight focused at all times."

"That's when I use mini-aids," Cam said.

Carole knew quite well that aids referred to the means a rider has of signaling the horse, specifically legs (and feet), hands (on the reins), and riding crop. She didn't know what Cam meant by mini-aids, though.

"It's sort of signaling the horse, but not really. You move the reins just a teeny little bit, alternating from side to side, or you touch his belly with your heels, ever so slightly. It's a way of saying, 'Hey, I'm here and I'm in charge, remember me?' "

"Of course," Carole said. "I've used that technique. It usually makes a horse much more alert and responsive. I should have thought of it while we were in the ring. In fact, I should probably train Starlight to use something like that on me so my mind doesn't wander, either!"

Cam smiled. "Sure," he said. "Just teach him to give you a little kick every now and then, huh?"

A picture flashed through Carole's mind of Starlight hiking up a hind leg and tapping her gently. It made her laugh. Cam laughed as well.

"Thanks," she said.

"I'm glad to help. I wish I could have helped before the class began."

"Don't worry," Carole said. "Stevie deserved her blue for that one. My turn is coming up."

"Oh, you think so?" Cam asked. "And what about me?"

There was a twinkle in his eye, but Carole wasn't entirely sure he was joking. She was pretty sure he was challenging her. "Are you going to be sorry you gave me such a good hint?" she teased.

"Not at all," he said. "I think it's good for us to be on equal ground. When I beat you, I want it to be fair and square."

"Beat me? Did I hear you say *beat* me? You actually think you're going to win in the Pleasure class?"

Cam was working on a good comeback when Stevie arrived. "Hi, guys," she said, looking back and forth quickly between them as if trying to figure out exactly what was going on.

"Hey, congratulations, Stevie," Cam said, offering his hand.

Stevie shook it. "Has either of you seen Lisa?" she asked.

"No," Carole said. "The last I saw of her, she was storming out of the ring yanking at Prancer's lead as she went. Have you seen Prancer?"

"Sure, Prancer is in her stall, munching away on some hay I just gave her. Apparently Lisa was too upset to think about Prancer's food and water. I took care of it."

"I can't blame her," Cam said. "She seemed upset even before her horse kicked the judge. I couldn't tell what was going on."

"Neither could we," Stevie said. Cam gave her an odd look. Carole filled him in on how Prancer came to be at Pine Hollow.

"She definitely needs more training before she's ready to be in a horse show," Carole said.

"Lisa?" Cam asked.

"No, not Lisa. Prancer. She's a retired racehorse, not a show horse. Yet."

"She's beautiful," Cam said.

"Agreed, but that's not enough," Stevie observed. All three of them knew that was true.

Then the public-address system kicked on again.

"The Intermediate Pleasure class will commence in ten minutes. Ten minutes. All riders must be mounted and in the East ring in five minutes. *Five Minutes!*"

"Let's go!" Stevie said.

"And may the best man win," Cam said, looking at Carole significantly.

"Woman," Carole and Stevie corrected him in a single voice.

"Person?" he suggested sheepishly.

"Woman," they said again.

"We'll see," Cam said, laughing.

CAROLE COULDN'T BELIEVE the difference in Starlight. It was as if he understood that he'd made a mistake in the last class and this time he wanted to make up for it. Carole used Cam's suggestions, and Starlight responded immediately. He was being the joy he usually was when they rode together. He did everything she wanted, exactly when she wanted him to do it. The Pleasure class was going beautifully, and Carole was very excited.

She was too excited to notice that Stevie was having a hard time. Just before the starter told Stevie it was time to go into the ring, Stevie had a flash of a recollection, remembering how unbelievably wonderful it had been to win a blue ribbon and gallop around the ring.

First prize, she whispered to herself, liking the sound of it. She glanced at the other competitors. Just a few minutes earlier Stevie might have thought of them as classmates, fellow riders, maybe even friends. As she entered the ring, however, she found herself thinking of them in another way: competitors. Even her best friend was in competition with her. Carole didn't know yet how wonderful it was to win a blue ribbon. Right then, Stevie didn't care if she ever found out. As far as Stevie was concerned, the only person in the world who should ever win another blue ribbon was Stevie Lake. And Topside. Then she remembered that that was what Phil had said—that she'd do better than her friends. It had made her feel a little uncomfortable when he'd said it, but now she felt as determined as she had ever been. She was determined to win this blue and every other one. She would take the championship. She would do it.

"You're up!" the starter declared, smiling brightly at Stevie. It was her turn. She was ready.

She gave Topside a kick, and the two of them entered the ring once more.

FROM HER VANTAGE point in the stable loft, Lisa saw it all. She saw Carole, a glow of joy on her face, now in complete control of her horse and glorying in every minute of the Pleasure class. It really looked as if riding were a pleasure for her, unlike the way it had seemed in the previous class.

Stevie, on the other hand, was having a terrible time. She had a dark and determined look on her face, and it seemed as though Topside were doing all the work. Lisa was surprised to realize that Stevie was simply trying too hard. Her body was stiff and nonresponsive. It looked as if Stevie was doing one thing and Topside another. They were in different riding classes! The one thing Stevie didn't seem to be doing was having a good time, and that was what the Pleasure class was about.

Lisa's eyes went to the judges' stand. She could see that the judges were talking about Stevie. One shook his head. This was a bad sign. Lisa didn't realize that the judge who'd shaken his head was the same judge who had excused her from the ring. It did not occur to Lisa that the head shake was anything but a fair judgment of the mistakes that Stevie was making. The judges felt sorry for Stevie. So did Lisa. The difference between Lisa and the judges was that Lisa knew what was wrong and wanted to tell her friend. Then Lisa realized that there was no reason why she shouldn't tell her friend. Maybe it would be too late for this class, but it wouldn't be too late for the next one. Stevie was good. She could win. She just had to remember that she *was* good and let Topside do the work he'd been so well trained to do.

It was no surprise when Carole took the blue in the Pleasure class. Cam came in second. Stevie came in sixth. She was almost as angry coming back out of the ring as Lisa had been when she'd been excused. However, the difference, as Lisa saw it, was that Stevie hadn't been doing a good job. She deserved to come in sixth.

Lisa left her perch on the hay bales and hurried down the narrow staircase of the loft to the main floor of the stable. She dashed out from the dark stable and ran into the temporary housing. She knew she would find Stevie by Topside's stall. And there she was.

Stevie had a steely look on her face. One thing about Stevie, when she was unhappy, there was no hiding it. She was definitely unhappy.

"Oh, Stevie!" Lisa began.

"What do you want?" her friend asked coldly.

"I saw it," Lisa said.

"You saw me blow it, you mean?"

"I saw you make a mistake," Lisa said. "That's all it was—a mistake."

"I blew it," Stevie said. "I got one blue ribbon, and all of a sudden I think I'm the champion of the world —that I'll get every blue ribbon there is. Well, I won't. I didn't. I was kidding myself. I'm no good."

"That's not true!" Lisa told her. "You're very good and Topside is, too! You just made a mistake."

"And *you* know what it was?" Stevie challenged.

"Well, sure," Lisa said, surprised that Stevie would even doubt it.

"All of a sudden, you're an expert?"

"I didn't say that. I just said I knew what you did wrong."

"Maybe, but don't bother to tell me. It won't make any difference. The judges aren't going to change their minds."

"Maybe not for this class, but you can do better in the next one," Lisa said.

"You think I'm going to go out there again, after that experience? I go from a blue ribbon to sixth place, and then I'm going to go for it again?"

"But of course!" Lisa said, astonished to realize that Stevie was ready to pack it in. "You have to!"

"Says who?"

Stevie had a sharp tongue, and she was using it. Lisa didn't care, though. She loved Stevie too much to let her make a mistake like this one. Just because she'd done poorly in one class didn't mean she could just quit. Lisa told her as much.

"Look, the trouble was that you were trying too hard. You completely forgot to have fun—"

"It wasn't fun," Stevie said icily.

"Well maybe not, but that doesn't mean you can't *look* like it's fun. You're good at pretending, Stevie, and I just know that when you get into the next class, you'll remember to relax, and then you will have fun. The next class is the Trail class. Trail riding has always been something you've enjoyed a lot. All you have to do is pretend that you are in the woods behind Pine Hollow—you'll do great!"

"You mean it, don't you?" Stevie asked.

Lisa nodded. She did mean it. She couldn't stand the idea that her friend Stevie was going to be a quitter.

"You really think I can do better?"

"Honestly, I do," Lisa said.

Stevie looked over at her horse. "What about you, Topside? Think we can improve from sixth place this time?"

Later both girls swore that Topside nodded. It was a small nod, but it was a nod. He was a very smart horse.

"All right. I'll take your advice," Stevie conceded. "I'll try again. I won't quit. On one condition."

"And that is?"

"That you take your own advice, too."

"Me?" Lisa asked. But she saw that she was speaking to thin air because Stevie had walked away toward the tack room mumbling something about saddle soap.

"Me?" Lisa said, echoing herself. She sighed. She couldn't imagine what Stevie was talking about.

11

THE STABLING AREA suddenly filled with riders, grooms, family members, and interested onlookers. The Pleasure riding class was finished, and that meant there was a half-hour break before the Trail class. There would be a general lunch break after that, and then the only class in the afternoon was jumping.

Lisa was concentrating so hard on Stevie's words that she didn't notice her mother approaching.

"Well, dear, how's it going?" Mrs. Atwood asked brightly. "I got a schedule and it looks like—what's the matter?"

Seeing her mother reminded Lisa of all the things that had happened to her in the awful morning that was now almost done. She'd been waiting for Mrs. Atwood to arrive and take her home. Ever since the judge had excused her, she'd wanted her mother to be there. There was something about a mother at a difficult time that nothing else could replace. Lisa knew she could count on her mother to take her side. Her mother would understand that what the judge had done wasn't fair. Her mother would comfort her and make it all better.

Without a word, and unable at that moment to describe how awful the morning had been, Lisa simply held out her arms and let her mother give her a comforting hug. Mrs. Atwood's arms surrounded her daughter, gave her warmth, love, and support—just what Lisa needed.

The tears came again then, flooding down Lisa's cheeks and onto her mother's shoulder.

"My dear, dear, Lisa. What *is* going on?" Mrs. Atwood asked, holding her daughter tightly. She patted Lisa's shoulder, just as she had a thousand times since Lisa had been an infant. It felt very loving and caring.

When Lisa thought she could talk, she led her mother to a quiet corner outside the stalls. She didn't want everybody in the world overhearing what she had to say. They had all seen her humiliation. They didn't need to hear about it.

The story flooded out just as the tears had.

". . . and then, when the judge ran her hands down Prancer's leg, Prancer just up and bucked, kicking the judge and knocking her down. I was excused.

We were both sent out of the ring. 'Disqualified,' was the word they used. It was *awful*!"

"The judge ran her hand down the horse's leg?" Mrs. Atwood said in surprise. "Well no wonder the horse bucked! What right did the judge have to do that? She must have had it in for you. There certainly is no excuse to send you out of the ring for something your horse did, and it's clear that the judge did something very improper. I mean what did she think—"

"It wasn't really improper, Mom," Lisa said. "The judges do that to all the horses. It's a way of checking the horse's conformation and making sure she's in good condition."

"It is? But it must be very annoying to the horse!"

"She did it to all the other horses," Lisa said. "None of them seemed to mind it."

"Well, she must have done it wrong to your beautiful horse," said Mrs. Atwood. "Otherwise, just give me one good reason why your horse would have felt it necessary to hurt her."

"I don't know, Mom. Prancer has always been a little odd and unreliable around adults. We don't know why that is, but it's just a character trait of hers. If the judge had been a young person, maybe Prancer wouldn't have done that."

"Well, why didn't they have a young judge for Prancer then?" Mrs. Atwood asked.

What a crazy idea, Lisa thought. How could her mother expect the whole show to adjust to her horse's peculiarity?

"It's not their job to have a special judge for a horse," Lisa said, speaking more sharply than she would have expected herself to. "It's the rider's job to have the horse ready to be inspected by the judge."

"But your horse was ready," Mrs. Atwood said. "I know you groomed her more carefully than anybody else, and she's so beautiful!"

"She is that," Lisa said. "She's the most beautiful horse I've ever seen. But beauty isn't all that goes into being fit for a horse show. She has to have manners, too. Prancer doesn't have her manners yet."

"Manners? Of course she doesn't have manners," Mrs. Atwood said. "How can they expect a young rider like you to teach a horse manners *and* control a horse? The judges are out of their minds if they blame *you* for something your horse does! I think I'll give them a piece of my mind! Just where can I find these so-called judges?"

On one hand, it was wonderful. Mrs. Atwood was doing exactly what Lisa had known she would do and had thought she needed her mother to do. She was supporting Lisa against everybody else. On the other hand, Mrs. Atwood's ideas of what was important in a horse show were so far off kilter that Lisa just had to try to explain. She couldn't have her mother going and telling the judges that they had been mean to Lisa! And with that thought, Lisa's vision of what had happened began to change. She didn't realize how much it changed until she heard her own voice speak the undeniable truth.

"No, no, Mom. You don't understand," Lisa said. "It is the job of somebody showing a horse to keep the horse under control. All the other riders managed it. I should have been able to do it, too. She's a beautiful, wonderful horse, but she is young and inexperienced. She hasn't learned good manners. She needs to learn them. She can't be allowed to misbehave all the rest of her life. A horse needs to learn manners, or it can't be trusted. A horse that can't be trusted shouldn't come to a horse show." Lisa could hardly believe what she'd just said and when she thought about it, she couldn't believe she hadn't said it earlier!

Mrs. Atwood looked puzzled. "But Prancer is so valuable!" she said. "I mean, isn't she a Thoroughbred racehorse?"

"Valuable?" Lisa echoed. She nodded. She was thinking. She was thinking hard for the first time since she'd heard about Briarwood. And, she realized, she was beginning to follow her own advice to Stevie. She wasn't thinking like a quitter.

"Yes, she's valuable, in a way," Lisa said. "That means she's an expensive horse—or that somebody probably paid a lot of money for her at one time. But she's not a racehorse anymore, Mom. She's retired from the track, so I can't really call her a valuable racehorse. She's got a weak bone in her foot that would certainly be passed on to any offspring, so she's not a valuable brood mare. She's got excellent conformation and tremendous potential as a show horse or a hunter—"

"Potential? I thought she was a champion."

"I thought so, too," said Lisa. "But I was wrong. She isn't a champion, yet. She will be. She definitely will be, but she isn't yet. Right now, she's like . . ." Lisa struggled, trying to think how to convey to her mother what had gone wrong. At the same time that she wanted to describe what had gone wrong with the horse, she needed to understand what had gone wrong with herself. Prancer had made mistakes, but Lisa understood that she had made the biggest mistakes of all. ". . . She's like a young girl who's never been in a horse show before and who doesn't understand what's really important until she loses it. I was wrong, Mom," Lisa said. "I thought that being in a horse show is about winning and that Prancer was the secret to winning. Now I know that Prancer wasn't ready to show. I had no business bringing such a green horse into a show ring. I'm lucky the judge didn't get badly hurt. Prancer could have kicked hard enough to break some bones! I must have been out of my mind!"

Lisa looked at her mother and shook her head in sorrow. She could tell that her mother didn't understand. Her mother could offer her comfort and support, but her mother just didn't understand about horses and horse shows. Lisa thought it wasn't all that surprising that her mother didn't understand, though, since she herself had only recently—like in the last two minutes—come to see what this was really about.

Mrs. Atwood offered her arms for comfort once again.

"Thanks for listening, Mom," Lisa said, accepting the hug and knowing that it was the only thing her mother could do for her.

"I'm just sorry for you, dear. Now let me take you home. Your dad will be home in a little while. You can take a nice hot bath, and then maybe we'll go to a movie. . . ."

Home? There was something inviting about a steaming bubbly bath and the comfort of the love and support of her parents, but Lisa knew that wasn't what she needed. She had work to do right here.

"I can't do it, Mom," she said. "I have to stay here."

"Why? There's nothing here for you, is there?"

"Maybe not me," Lisa said. "But there is something for my friends, and I want to be here for them. Stevie and Carole are both doing well in the show. I'm going to stick around and cheer them on."

That was right. It sounded right and it felt right. It was the first *right* idea Lisa had had since the moment she had chosen Prancer for the horse show.

"But how will you get home?"

"Max will bring me," she said. "Or maybe Stevie's parents. Don't worry. I'll find a way."

Lisa was a little startled then to find that Max was standing behind her. "No problem, Mrs. Atwood. I'll bring her home," he said. "Lisa's right to stay. She's got some work to do."

"I do?"

"Yes, you do," he said.

"Well, I have these tickets," Mrs. Atwood said.

"Maybe I'll just stay around here and watch some of the horse show. It seems that there are a lot of things about horse shows I don't understand. I might learn something watching."

"Yes, you might," Max agreed. "There's a lot of learning going on here today." Then he told Mrs. Atwood where he'd seen some empty seats, and she left to find them.

Lisa spoke before he had a chance to say anything. "I really blew it, didn't I?"

He smiled at the way she'd put it. "Yes, I think you did. But I knew your mind was made up. It reminded me of a time I was just determined to ride a new horse that Dad brought into the stable. His name was Lightning, I think. He was a beauty, too, and I just had to take him out on a trail ride. . . ."

Lightning? That was the name of the horse in the story Mrs. Reg had told Lisa. That meant that the story was about Max!

"You were in the hospital?" Lisa asked.

Max stopped talking and looked at her in surprise. Then he understood. "Do I gather that my mother has beat me to the punch on this story?"

Lisa nodded. "I guess you and I have something in common."

"Sure," Max agreed. "It means we've both done things we should have known better than to do. And it appears that we've both learned from the experience."

He put his arm across her shoulder and gave her a

hug. It wasn't a warm maternal hug, the way her mother had hugged her, but it was a very important one. Max's hug told her that she, Lisa, was going to be able to make everything all right for herself.

"Thanks," she said to Max. "I needed that. Now I think my friends need me. I'm going to go help them get ready for the Trail class."

"No, there's something else you need to do," Max said, stopping her midtrack.

"What?"

"Well, according to the Briarwood rules, your disqualification applied to Prancer, not necessarily to you. I would like to see you compete in the last two Intermediate classes here today."

"Me, too," Lisa agreed. "But I think the Briarwood rules require that I be on the back of some sort of four-footed animal. . . ."

"Like Barq?" Max said.

"Barq?"

"Sure. We brought him because one of the adults is going to ride him later in the Senior Jumping class. Until then, he's available for any rider who might consider petitioning the judges to permit her to ride a new horse. It's the sort of thing that would be permitted if a horse became lame. That's just another kind of disqualification."

"How do I petition? I mean, do I have to sign something?"

Max's eyes flicked around until they found what he was looking for. He pointed to a place where the three

116

Intermediate judges were standing and chatting during the break. "I think all you have to do is to go ask nicely. See if you can do it without kicking anybody, okay?" he teased. Then he gave her a gentle, encouraging shove.

A half hour later, Lisa was back in the saddle, this time mounted on Barq, and all ready to compete in the Trail class.

Veronica had given her a nasty look, and that made Lisa feel good. Even better, though, Stevie and Carole had given her high fives when she'd shared her exciting news. Even the judge who'd been kicked by Prancer seemed pleased. She'd wished Lisa good luck. Max clapped loudly when she entered the ring. Her mother waved with excitement. Mrs. Reg smiled. But best of all was the way Lisa felt about herself. No matter what happened for the rest of the day, Lisa understood that she was a winner.

12

BARQ WAS A wonderful horse. Lisa had ridden the bay gelding before and had just forgotten how nice it was to give a horse an instruction and have him follow it. There was an exciting feeling of freedom, and Barq sensed her joy. The two of them worked in near-perfect union for the entire class.

In the Trail class, the ring had been set up with a path each rider had to follow in turn, with small obstacles along the way. There were no jumps, as there would be in the actual Jumping class, but poles and cones had been set out to simulate a crooked trail with various natural objects that a horse and rider would have to maneuver around.

Barq seemed to think it was a lot of fun to follow the circuitous trail and step gingerly over the poles and the pan of water that had been laid out as a "creek." Barq especially liked the creek. Lisa wondered if it actually reminded him of Willow Creek, which wandered through the woods behind Pine Hollow. She would never know, but what she did know was that her horse accepted the challenge and met every turn and obstacle like the fine trail horse he was.

When she'd finished riding the "course," Lisa found she didn't care a bit whether or not she won a ribbon or even placed. She'd competed. She'd had fun. That was all that mattered.

She watched as the other riders followed the trail. Some were better than others. Veronica and Garnet had some trouble because Veronica wasn't paying enough attention. When Garnet stopped to take a drink out of the "creek," Lisa knew she was out of the running for a ribbon. That didn't bother Lisa at all.

Carole and Starlight had fun, just the way Lisa had. Starlight seemed to like events that didn't require perfect attention the way Equitation did. He moved easily and gracefully among the obstacles, and Carole was pleased with his performance.

Lisa was very glad to see that Stevie and Topside were back in top form, too. This wasn't going to be Topside's best event because, in a way, Topside was the complete opposite of Starlight. Topside was at his best when total structure was called for. That was what his training was. He was good at trail riding and he enjoyed it, but his heart was in dressage, and that was where he excelled. Still, he was doing pretty well, and Stevie, at least, looked as if she were enjoying herself. Actually, when Lisa caught her attention briefly, Stevie winked at her. That was a sure sign that Stevie was having fun. Lisa was glad she'd talked Stevie into continuing in the show. She was also glad that Stevie had told her to take her own advice, because that was just what she was doing.

When the ribbons were handed out, Lisa could hardly believe that she got a red one—second place! It seemed right, too, that Carole's friend, Cam, got the blue. He and Duffy had done a wonderful job on the trail and deserved the blue. Carole came in third. She seemed pleased by that, and Stevie took a fifth. Veronica didn't place at all. That seemed right, too.

Then it was lunchtime. It would give the young riders a chance to see what was going on in the Senior Division competition because the Seniors' lunch break would come later. It would also give the young riders—especially The Saddle Club—a chance to *talk*. And there was so much to talk about. The threesome, joined by Cam, bought hot dogs and sodas and walked around the whole area of the show.

The Junior riders (both Beginner and Intermediate) were using two rings off one end of the stable, whereas the Senior Division used several larger ones off the other end of the stable. The girls and Cam had spent all of their time so far with the young riders and hadn't even seen where the Seniors were performing. The four of them found a spot by the fence of the ring and watched a hunter-jumper class.

"Look at that form!" Cam said in frank admiration while one rider completed the course flawlessly. None of them was surprised when she took the blue ribbon in the event.

"What I have to do is learn to maintain an even pace the way that rider did," Carole said.

"Oh, I think you can do it," Cam told her. "Starlight moves so beautifully that he can certainly do it with an even pace. And how does he jump?"

"He's the best," Carole said enthusiastically. "He can jump very high, and it's like flying. In fact, sometimes the real trick is holding him back."

"Right. It's not good form for a horse to jump four feet high over a two-foot fence."

"It's better than the other way around," Stevie said philosophically.

All four of them laughed. To each, the tensions of the morning, the disappointments, the difficulties, and the stress of the hard lessons, seemed to drain away. They were thoroughly enjoying themselves while surrounded by the one thing they each loved the most: horses.

When the hunter-jumper class was finished, Lisa looked at her watch and informed the others that it was time for them to get back to the stalls. They needed to prepare for the last, and hardest, event of the day, Jumping class.

In the first three classes of the day, all of the competitors had been in the ring at the same time. The Trail class and Jumping class were different from those in that the competitors each performed separately, alone in the ring.

Stevie was the first of the four of them to go through the course. She leaned forward and gave Topside a reassuring pat on his neck before they entered the ring. Then she heard her name and Topside's announced. It was time to enter the ring and begin the course. Suddenly she was flooded with thoughts. She thought about how wonderful it had been to win a blue in Equitation and how awful it had been to do so badly in the Pleasure class. Then she recalled the feeling of relief when she'd done her best in the Trail class and placed just about where she'd thought she ought to place. It had been a long day, but she felt as if she'd come so far. Now all that was left was this. She and Topside could complete the course, and they could do it well. That's all she wanted. Not only would it be enough for her, but it would be wonderful.

She clucked her tongue and entered the ring, a big smile on her face. She was ready and set. It was time to go.

"See how nicely she's doing that!" Lisa said excitedly.

"She's on a great horse," Cam said.

"It's not the horse that's the most important. It's the rider," Lisa said. "It's the rider who has to make all the important decisions and the horse that has to be well enough trained to do the job."

"Very good!" Carole said, teasing. "This has been a productive day, hasn't it?"

Lisa smiled, knowing she deserved a little ribbing. "Yes, it has. Oh, there she goes again, flying over the jumps. Stevie's great!"

Then Stevie was finished. She rode out of the ring and straight over to her friends. Lisa and Carole both reached out to slap the hand she offered. It wasn't the same as the hug they wanted to give her, but it was the best they could do on horseback.

"Topside was in top form," Stevie said. "I'm pretty sure we'll place in this one."

"Of course you will," Carole said. Then, still in a teasing mood, she continued. "The only real question is which one of us, you or me, will take the blue!"

"Or me," Cam interjected.

Carole felt a little twinge of discomfort and confusion. She had found during the course of the day that she really liked Cam. He was a good rider. He knew a lot about horses, and he was generous with his knowledge. When she'd been writing to him, his generosity had sometimes sounded like showing off, but in person that wasn't it at all. He was just a nice person. In fact, he was more than just a nice person. It was one thing to joke with her friends about competition and blue ribbons, but was it okay to joke with Cam about it? Carole realized with a start then that her friendship with Cam might go further than a shared interest in horses. Could he, maybe, one day, be a *boyfriend*? Suddenly she was flooded with unfamiliar thoughts. If he was going to be a boyfriend, was it all right to joke and tease with him? Was it acceptable to want to beat him in the horse show? How about actually beating him? She wasn't sure how she felt—other than confused— and she wasn't sure what to do. Stevie solved the immediate problem for her.

"You've already had your blue," she said to Cam bluntly. "Now it's Carole's turn again. No horse in this ring is a better jumper than Starlight anyway."

"She's right," Lisa piped in.

"Maybe," Cam said. "But that won't keep me from trying."

"I certainly hope it won't," Carole said, gaining the confidence she needed from her friends. "See, I want to beat you fair and square!"

He laughed, recalling that he'd used those very words on Carole. Then he offered his hand. "A deal," he said. They shook.

"Cam Nelson on Duffy!" the amplifier squeaked. It was Cam's turn.

The three girls watched every minute of Cam's performance, and it was very good.

"He really knows what he's doing," Lisa said.

"Yeah," Carole said. Stevie thought she sounded wistful, but dismissed the thought. There was no way Carole was going to go soft and mushy when the subject was horses. Horses were Carole's life. Then she had another thought: Was the subject horses or Cam? She glanced at Carole. The look on Carole's face gave Stevie a hint. Something was going on!

"Duffy's quite a horse," Lisa said. "Cam has really

trained him very well. Look how he keeps him alert and responsive all the time."

Carole focused on Cam's performance. He was using the same techniques he'd recommended to her that had worked so well for her in the Pleasure class. What a nice thing it had been for him to remind her about those mini-aids. It had definitely helped her.

Cam finished his round then and returned to where the girls were waiting for him.

"You're next," he said to Lisa.

She was, and she was ready. Jumping a horse was different from flat riding, and Lisa hadn't been jumping for very long. She didn't expect to do all that well here. She certainly didn't consider herself to be anywhere near as good as Stevie or Carole, but she did consider herself to be good enough to do her best and to make Barq do his best. That was all she asked of herself. Earlier in the day it would have been more than she could have done. Now she felt it was the right goal for herself. She gave Barq a nudge, and they began the course.

There were ten jumps, and the course involved a lot of tricky turns to navigate it correctly. It took every ounce of Lisa's concentration. She and Barq got to a nice smooth canter, aimed straight at the first jump. She never moved her eyes from it. Then, at just the right moment, she rose in the saddle, leaned forward, gave Barq some rein, and the two of them soared over it, landing smoothly. Barq never missed a beat of his canter.

"One down, nine to go," Lisa whispered to herself.

Barq understood. He knew what to do. He'd done it before, and he wasn't going to let her down now. The next jump was as smooth as the first. The third jump gave them some trouble. They went over it all right, but they weren't in the center of the jump, and Lisa was pretty sure that would cost them some points. The next two jumps were better, but after the sixth, Barq began hurrying. It was as if he could feel that this was almost over, and Lisa knew that she'd lost some of the control she had to keep in order to do well. She pulled in a little on the rein. Barq slowed down and then once again found his even pace. They completed the last three jumps successfully. They'd done well and Lisa was proud of it. She couldn't think of a time when she'd jumped a course of obstacles any better than what she'd just done with Barq. That was what it was about. That was how a rider succeeded in a horse show. She felt good and was glad to receive the congratulations from her friends when she got back out of the ring.

Stevie's round was very good. Again, this wasn't Topside's strongest class, but he was a good, solid jumper and Stevie was a good, solid rider. Topside's previous owner, Dorothy DeSoto, had ridden him in jumping competitions, but they were usually stadium jumping, where the height of the jumps and the speed of the round were more important than style. He was better at that than at hunter jumping, where style counted for almost everything. They did well, though, and they didn't make any obvious faults. Stevie was convinced the judges had noticed a lot of things she never would have noticed herself. She hoped she was wrong.

And then it was Carole's turn. She and Starlight were announced. Carole could feel the tension rise in her. She was nervous and she thought Starlight was, as well. She'd always thought this would be her best class. Starlight was a natural jumper. She was suddenly filled with doubts. Would she clutch the way Stevie had, or freeze as Lisa had? Would she slip and lose her attention and let Starlight's attention lag? Would she . . .

She didn't want to think about all the things that could go wrong, and very quickly she found that she didn't have time to think about those things anyway. She was in the ring. It was her turn.

As things worked out, it *was* Carole's turn. From the moment she first touched Starlight's belly and began her canter until the final jump had been cleared, everything went even better than Carole might have dreamed. Starlight and Carole rode the whole course as one, keeping a perfectly even pace, approaching each jump straight on, rising from the ground at exactly the right distance from the jump and landing so smoothly, Carole was sure she could have carried a glass of water with her and not spilled a drop. It was simply a dream ride.

Everybody in the audience knew it, too. Her father, Max, and Mrs. Reg stood up and clapped for her. Near them Carole saw that Lisa's mother was standing and clapping. Even the judges were smiling, though, of course, they weren't clapping. That would have been very bad form.

Carole felt totally numb as Starlight drew to a proper walk to leave the ring. She didn't even know where she was going, so it turned out to be a very good thing that Starlight thought he was ready for a good long drink of water and some hay. At least he knew where to find it!

"That was fabulous!" Stevie shrieked, leaning over from Topside to give Carole a hug.

"Totally!" Lisa agreed. She would have joined in on the hug, but it wasn't possible physically.

"Definitely," Cam added to Stevie and Lisa's congratulations. "It was far and away the best."

"Do you think so?" Carole asked. She really wasn't sure.

"Stop digging for compliments," Stevie said. "You're going to have a blue ribbon to prove us all right in just a minute, so wait quietly."

That was all right with Carole. It was all she could do anyway. She was still too exhilarated by the ride she and Starlight had taken.

There were two more riders after Carole, but the audience hardly noticed them. Everybody knew who had won the blue and who deserved it. Nobody was surprised and everyone was pleased when the judges announced their decision.

"First prize of a blue ribbon to Carole Hanson on Starlight!"

Starlight heard his name. He bounced alertly, and it was a good thing, too, because Carole almost didn't hear the announcement.

"Go on, girl. Get your prize!" Cam said. "You won it, you deserve it."

It was true. She had won the blue. She was only vaguely aware of the audience and the judges, and of the clapping and the cries and waves. She rode Starlight up to the judges' stand and waited patiently as the blue ribbon for the Jumping class was pinned on her horse.

"Second prize of a red ribbon to Cam Nelson and his horse, Duffy."

That was when Carole realized that she'd actually beaten Cam. They'd been joking about who would win, and she had won. For a second she felt bad, remembering how much she liked Cam and didn't want to hurt his feelings. The second passed, though. She and Starlight had done a wonderful job on the course and deserved to win. Cam had been good. He deserved second place.

Then, in an instant of recognition, Carole realized she was glad she had beaten Cam. She liked him as a friend and might like him as a boyfriend, but she would never like him at all if she couldn't feel free to be her best around him. That included joking, teasing, and trying to win. That realization was a wonderful feeling of freedom for Carole.

And then there was more good news because Stevie got third place and Lisa took the fourth-place ribbon.

When the other ribbons had been awarded and Carole had taken her victory gallop, the judges called all of the Intermediate riders into the ring on their horses. Carole wasn't certain what was going on, but the grin on Cam's face told her it was good.

One of the judges stood up to the microphone and began a long explanation. It took Carole and her friends a few seconds to catch the idea, but it had to do with champion and reserve champion. Carole had completely forgotten about those awards. They were intended as sort of overall recognition of the best horse and rider in the group of classes. There was a point system. At this show, championship points were earned by the top five placers in each class. First place got five points, second place four points, and so on.

Carole's mind raced. She had two blues. That was ten points. But then, she hadn't done well at all in Equitation and only got a fourth in Fitting and Showing.

"One of the purposes of this championship system is that it sometimes enables us to recognize a rider who does consistently well, but may only take, for example, one blue ribbon. That's the case here today.

"We are pleased to award the championship ribbon to the rider who acquired twenty-one points, and that is Cam Nelson on Duffy!"

Cam! How wonderful. Sure, Carole had done better than he had in two classes, but he'd done well in all of the classes, and he deserved something more than one blue ribbon. Carole thought that was just great. She and her friends and everybody in the audience clapped long and loudly for Cam as the bright multicolored ribbon was clipped onto Duffy's bridle.

Carole started to signal Starlight to return to the stable. She could hardly wait to congratulate Cam in person. It seemed so right—

"And the reserve championship goes to the rider who acquired eighteen points, and that is Carole Hanson on Starlight!"

Me?

"Yahoo!" Stevie said.

Carole hadn't even known there was such a thing as a reserve championship, and now she'd won it. She and Starlight accepted the ribbon, and then she and Cam were invited to ride around the ring together.

Carole couldn't remember when she'd had such fun on such a short ride. Together they circled the ring, and then together they left the competition area for the stalls, followed by all the other Intermediate competitors.

As soon as they were inside, Carole dismounted and gave Starlight the gigantic hug that he deserved. She also took the opportunity to congratulate Cam and tell him how much she thought he deserved it.

"Thanks," he said. "I'm glad for you, too."

Then both of them were surrounded. All the young riders seemed happy for both Carole and Cam, but none were happier for them than Lisa and Stevie.

"It's great!" Lisa declared.

"It's Saddle Club Power!" Stevie said, reaching up and inviting Carole and Lisa to join her in a high five —only when there were three of them, they called it a high fifteen.

"What exactly do you three do in The Saddle Club, anyway?" Cam asked.

"Haven't I told you about our meetings?" Carole asked.

"I've got an idea," Stevie said, reaching to take Starlight's reins from Carole's hands. "Why don't Lisa and I untack your horses—it will be an honor to tend to the champ and the reserve champ—while you two go somewhere private and Carole can explain to Cam what The Saddle Club is."

"Good idea," Lisa agreed, taking Duffy's reins. "And if, when you come back, you've got something cool for each of us to drink, well that will be fine, too."

"It's a deal," Cam said. "Oh, but be sure to take good care of Duffy. He's a champion, you know."

"Don't worry," Lisa said. "I'm good at grooming champions—and champions-to-be!"

Cam took Carole's hand then and led her out toward the refreshment stand. They had a lot to talk about, and Stevie and Lisa suspected it wasn't all horses!

13

"WE WERE WONDERFUL!" Stevie declared. She was sitting in the big easy chair in Carole's room with her slippered feet propped up on Carole's bed. The three of them were having a hastily arranged sleepover. It was a celebration of the victories they'd had at the horse show. It was also a Saddle Club meeting, because every time the three of them got together without any other distractions (and sometimes *with* other distractions), they called it a Saddle Club meeting.

"We sure were wonderful," Lisa said. "Especially Carole."

"Thanks," Carole said. "It was a very special day, that's for sure."

The three of them were quiet for a few minutes then, each lost in her own thoughts.

133

"For a while there, all I cared about was winning," Stevie said. "I kind of assumed that was the only important part of the horse show."

"And I assumed that just because I had a valuable horse, I would win everything," Lisa said. "I was such a dope."

"You weren't a dope," Carole said quickly. "You were just acting like one!"

The three girls laughed because they all knew that what Carole had said was true.

"And besides," she went on, "I did my part in acting like a dope, too. Talking about assuming things, how about the way I assumed Cam was a girl? Boy did I miss the boat on that one!"

"He's not only a boy, he's a nice boy," Lisa said. "He tried to help me when I was messing up with Prancer."

"He *is* a nice boy," Carole agreed. "He helped me, too. And now that I know how nice he is, I'm going to listen more carefully to his advice. It was silly of me to assume that I knew more than anybody else on my bulletin board."

Stevie frowned. "Does that mean you're always going to take his advice?" she asked. It was hard to imagine Carole relinquishing her position as an expert on horses.

"Heavens no!" Carole said. "I didn't say he was always right—just that he's worth listening to."

That was more like it!

"Then there was another way that I acted like a

134

dope," Carole continued in a more serious vein. "I mean, I got frazzled when Starlight gave me such trouble in the Equitation class. I'd assumed that just because he and I had worked so hard, we'd do well. I found that working hard might help in some areas, but in others I'm just going to have to work harder."

"My dopiness had to do with the fact that I thought determination would win," Stevie said. "All I wanted to do was to win. I thought I could beat you both and I thought that would make me happy. I was wrong on both counts. I can be so competitive sometimes!"

"Right, and all that did was make you look determined, and that wasn't what the judges wanted to see in the Pleasure class. Now if there had been a Determination class . . . ," Lisa teased.

"It all worked out, though, didn't it?" Stevie asked. "I mean, we all won something."

"If you mean ribbons, yes," Lisa agreed. "And we probably got those in the right proportions, too. We're each pretty good riders, but nobody's kidding anybody here. Carole's the best, Stevie, you're next best, and I'm . . ." She paused for a moment, trying to think of a flattering way to describe the fact that she wasn't as good a rider as her friends. Then she had it. ". . . I'm learning the most!" she declared.

"Lucky you!"

Lisa continued on a more serious note. "Well, there was a lot to learn today. I think we all got something out of the show."

"You know, that's what Max said he wanted for us,"

Carole said, recalling their first talk with Max about Briarwood. "He said he wanted students who could learn at the show, and then later he said it again when he was talking about our personal goals."

"Oh, those," Stevie said. "I'd forgotten. We're supposed to meet with Max on Tuesday, and he'll tell us how we did."

Carole shook her head. "No, you've got it wrong," she said. "We're supposed to tell *him* how we did—what ribbon we're supposed to get. What are you two going to say?"

Stevie scrunched her forehead. "I'm trying to remember what I wrote down. I was afraid that Topside was going to make it all so easy for me that I wouldn't do the job I was supposed to do. I wanted to stay concentrated on the basics."

"That's a good goal," Carole said. "I wish I'd thought of it that way. So do you think you did it?"

Stevie shrugged. "Most of the time, I guess I did. I certainly didn't do it in the Pleasure class, but I did okay the rest of the time."

"You should get a blue ribbon then," Lisa said.

"No, I don't agree," Stevie told her earnestly. "Red is good enough for me this time." Then she turned to Carole. "What about you? What were your goals?"

"I don't remember all of them, although I thought about them a lot when I wrote them down. Most of them had to do with making Starlight do his best because we'd worked so hard on his training for so long."

"And what are you going to say to Max?" Lisa asked.

Carole thought for a while before she answered the question. "This may sound odd, or it may sound conceited. I don't know which you might think, but the fact is that Starlight *did* do his best all through the show. Sometimes it wasn't as good as I had hoped it would be, but I know Starlight's limitations, and I'm very sure I got the best he had to give me. I'm going to tell Max I earned a blue."

Stevie and Lisa both had the same thought. From almost anybody else in the world, that would have sounded like a boast. From Carole it was the honest truth, and they couldn't fault her. She'd done so well that she clearly deserved at least one more blue ribbon. They told her so. She thanked them.

Then both Stevie and Carole turned to Lisa. "What were your goals?" Carole asked.

Lisa shifted uneasily and made a face. She remembered exactly what she'd written on each of those five pieces of paper. The recollection was embarrassing to her because it had been so foolish to think she could win blue ribbons with a horse who needed so much more training than Prancer had. But she wasn't quite ready to explain it all to her friends.

She took a deep breath and tried, in the best way she could. "Well, with my envelope it seems that there was some kind of mistake," she began. "The 'goals' that got written down for this year are actually 'goals' that were meant for next year—or, maybe about fifteen years from now, when I'm a lot older and wiser."

Stevie and Carole didn't ask for any details. They understood, and that was what friends were for.

"And speaking of goals," Stevie said. "Tell us about your conversation with Cam after you left us. You were gone an awfully long time when you went to get those drinks for us. Just what kind of questions did Cam ask you about The Saddle Club?"

"Oh, we didn't talk about The Saddle Club at all," Carole said.

"Well, did he ask you anything?" said Lisa.

"Sure," Carole said. Her friends thought there was a possibility that she was blushing as she answered the question. "He did ask me one question."

"Yes?"

"He asked me my phone number." Carole smiled shyly. "And I gave it to him."

"Wow!" Stevie said. This was great news. Cam Nelson seemed like such a nice boy. "He's so handsome, and such a good rider! You guys are perfect for one another! When are you going to see him?"

"Oh, I don't know—" Carole began.

Then there was a knock at her door. It was Carole's father. Colonel Hanson had a big tray of cookies and milk for the three girls.

"I thought all you ribbon winners deserved to be waited on just a little tiny bit," he said. "So here are some homemade chocolate-chip cookies." He put the tray on Carole's bedside table and began handing out the milk. "Of course, in return I am going to expect breakfast in bed from you three tomorrow morning. I like my eggs boiled for three and a half minutes—no, actually three minutes forty-five seconds. . . ."

Lisa began giggling. Colonel Hanson was a wonderful man, and he could be very funny. He often made the girls laugh. Stevie didn't giggle. She just tossed a pillow at him—when he wasn't holding a glass of milk in his hand.

"All right, all right. Just burn me some toast, okay?"

"It's a deal," Carole said.

"Well, now, I have a question for you, daughter dear. Now that you've won a reserve championship, two blue ribbons, and countless lesser ones, what are you going to do next?"

Carole got a little twinkle in her eye. She shrugged casually. "I'm going to go to Disney World!"

Colonel Hanson's jaw dropped. "How did you know?" he asked.

There was a *lot* to talk about!

ABOUT THE AUTHOR

BONNIE BRYANT is the author of more than fifty books for young readers, including novelizations of movie hits such as *Teenage Mutant Ninja Turtles* and *Honey, I Shrunk the Kids*, written under her married name, B. B. Hiller.

Ms. Bryant began writing The Saddle Club in 1986. Although she had done some riding before that, she intensified her studies then and found herself learning right along with her characters Stevie, Carole, and Lisa. She claims that they are all much better riders than she is.

Ms. Bryant was born and raised in New York City. She lives in Greenwich Village with her two sons.